Lines of Loyalty

Torn Between Duty and Desire

HOUSE OF
STARLYND

By

Starlynd Rivers

Copyright

Copyright © 2025 Starlynd Rivers

Published by

Dedication

For the unapologetic seekers of truth, the keepers of tomorrow's hope, and the loyal hearts who know that every lock has its key.

Acknowledgement

Stories begin with a single spark, and this one has carried me further than I ever imagined. Writing *Lines of Loyalty* has been both a challenge and a gift, and though it is my debut novel, it feels like the first step on a much longer path—one I am grateful you've chosen to walk with me.

To every reader who opened these pages: thank you. Your belief in stories, in love, in resilience, is what transforms words on a page into something living. Without you, this book would remain only ink and silence. With you, it finds its voice.

The House of Starlynd has always been more than an idea—it is a vision, a key, a feather, a chest. It is the belief that courage, truth, and love will always find a way forward. My hope is that this story is just one ember among many, lighting sparks that carry into tomorrow.

And to tomorrow itself—thank you for its promise. For second chances. For unrelenting truth. For fires that burn brighter in the darkness. This is not an ending. It is the beginning.

Author's Note

When I first sat down to write *Lines of Loyalty*, I thought I was simply chasing a story about power, corruption, and politics. But somewhere along the way, it became more than that. It became about courage when silence would be safer. About loyalty when betrayal is easier. About finding love in the middle of danger and realizing that sometimes the fight for truth is also a fight for your own heart.

This book is my debut, and writing it has been both terrifying and exhilarating. Every page carried pieces of me—the doubts, the persistence, the quiet hope that someone out there might see themselves reflected in Elena's determination or in Logan's relentless will to protect what matters.

If you are holding this book in your hands, I want to thank you. Your time and trust mean the world to me. Stories don't live without readers; they don't breathe without someone stepping inside their world. Thank you for stepping into this one.

Most of all, know this: while *Lines of Loyalty* tells its own story, it's only the beginning. The fire continues to burn, and the truth will demand to be heard in what comes next.

With gratitude and hope,

Starlynd Rivers

Table of Content

Chapter 1: Shadows in the Capitol

The grand corridors of the Capitol thrummed with quiet urgency, sunlight sliding across the polished marble floors like liquid silver beneath Elena Delgado's purposeful stride. Her heels clicked sharply, echoing off the walls in a rhythmic pulse that mirrored her steady resolve. Yet beneath the surface of her confident gait, a cold prickle traced the nape of her neck—a silent warning she'd carried ever since she began exposing the rot of Donovan's corrupt empire.

"Elena, five minutes until your meeting," Valerie called out, hurrying slightly to keep pace. Her voice was steady but edged with concern. "Then there's the briefing. I'll text you the files so you can review them beforehand."

"Thanks, Val," Elena replied, her voice calm but taut. Her eyes flicked involuntarily toward the long shadows pooling in the marble hallway's corners. The Capitol had long been her fortress, a place of control and authority. But now, each step through these halls felt like walking deeper into a trap— not a sanctuary, but a gauntlet riddled with unseen threats.

A sudden buzz in her pocket shattered her thoughts. She glanced down at the screen: an unknown number blinking insistently. Her breath caught, hesitation pinning her for a heartbeat before she answered. "Congresswoman Delgado."

Silence stretched—cold, expectant.

Then, the voice came, distorted and harsh, crackling like static through the line: "Stop digging, or you'll regret it."

The line went dead.

Elena froze mid-stride, her pulse pounding, the threat sinking in like ice beneath her calm exterior. Valerie's hand settled firmly on her arm—steady, reassuring.

"Elena? What is it?"

"Nothing," she lied smoothly, forcing her voice into a measured calm as she slipped the phone back into her pocket. "Let's keep moving."

But inside, her mind raced. The warnings had escalated. Whoever lurked behind them wasn't merely trying to intimidate—they meant to silence her. Permanently.

***

The meeting passed in a blur, a dull roar of voices washing over Elena Delgado as her attention splintered beneath the surface. She sat rigidly at the long-polished table, a pen suspended and useless above her notepad. Her thoughts spun relentlessly, tethered to the echo of that chilling phone call. The steady drone of discussion became white noise, fragmented by the occasional glance toward the clock on the pale wall—each tick a reminder of precious minutes slipping away, each second edging her closer to escape.

When the meeting finally adjourned, the words had barely registered, evaporating before they could settle.

"Congresswoman Delgado, do you have a moment?" A voice cut through her fog as she packed her papers, pulling her back to the moment.

She nodded absently, offering a polite, distracted reply before slipping through the doorway. The corridor beyond greeted her with a colder, heavier silence. It pressed down differently than the crowded room—a quiet that seemed to amplify the weight nesting in her chest.

Her fingers tightened around her phone as she walked, the screen glowing faintly with Valerie's briefing details. She read the contact's name—Logan Chase—but the rest blurred into static beneath the relentless playback of the threatening voice. Elena didn't scare easily; she had weathered countless storms in the Capitol's unforgiving halls. But this voice was different. It wasn't just a warning. It was a promise. Personal.

The briefing room loomed ahead, its door a threshold between polished certainty and shadowed unease. Thick curtains muted the waning sunlight, suffocating the space in cold half-light. The air was crisp, almost sterile, broken only by the faint hum of the working air conditioner, a low pulse under the oppressive quiet.

He stood by the window—Logan Chase. Broad, solid, his silhouette etched sharply against the dim glow. The coolness of the room brushed against her skin, but it failed to douse the fire stoking low in her chest—a smoldering ember she barely dared acknowledge. Even his mere outline held a magnetic pull, an unspoken warning she resisted yet could not ignore.

When he turned, the atmosphere shifted, charged and immediate. His piercing blue eyes bore into hers with a sharpness that narrowed the world to just this moment, just the two of them. The subtle scent of cologne—earthy, faintly leathery—wove through the space between them, mingling with an electric tension that made her breath hitch.

A single, stark thought echoed in her mind: He's trouble.

This wasn't the dry briefing she had braced herself for. This was a collision—raw, unpredictable. Beyond the firm set of his jaw and the controlled calm, there was a fire in his gaze, a silent dare that stirred something deep inside her—like the distant rumble of a storm on the horizon, waiting to break.

"Elena Delgado," he said, his voice steady, low, and sure, sending a jolt of heat coursing through her veins.

She resisted the instinct to recoil, meeting his unwavering gaze with the cool precision that had always been her armor. He was calm, professional—yet beneath the surface, something gnawed at her awareness, something raw and almost primal in his presence.

Her eyes fixed on his outstretched hand, her body tensing subtly as she weighed him. Was it his effortless confidence that filled the room, or something more elusive—a dangerous edge that made her skin prickle? The question flickered in her mind as if daring her to decide: step back, or step forward?

"I'm Logan Chase. Your new security detail." His voice cut through the thick stillness with quiet authority. Elena barely blinked, her expression a cool mask of detachment—an armor forged through years of navigating Capitol battles.

"I didn't request security," she said, her tone sharp as a blade slicing through the silence.

Her eyes flicked over him, appraising, calculating. He didn't flinch under her scrutiny. That should have ignited frustration, but instead, it sparked something deeper inside her—curiosity she wasn't ready to acknowledge. She had no use for bodyguards or anyone who tried to dictate what she needed. Control was hers alone.

His gaze held steady. "Your Chief of Staff disagreed," he replied evenly, the words deliberate. "I was sure they'd inform you." A subtle tension hummed around him—quiet but electric, like a coiled wire ready to snap. "Given the recent threats, this isn't optional. It's a necessity."

Elena crossed her arms deliberately—a shield raised not only in defense but in declaration. "I can handle myself," she said, voice resolute, eyes locked on him like a challenge.

He didn't waver. Instead, her stomach tightened as he took a measured step closer, shrinking the space between them. She didn't retreat—stepping back was never in her nature—but her heart betrayed her calm, quickening despite herself.

"Not against the kind of threats you're facing." His voice dropped lower, the firmness tinged now with something almost possessive, an unspoken claim. Elena's gaze flicked briefly to the folder he'd placed on the glossy table—it seemed to smolder there, daring her to confront its contents.

He continued; voice steady but heavy with warning: "I've reviewed your file. You've made enemies—powerful ones. They don't play by the rules."

Her eyes snapped back to his, steel meeting steel. "I don't need a babysitter," she shot back sharply, the edge in her voice mirroring the glare she fixed on him.

His jaw tightened, but he held firm. And then, a darker flicker appeared in his eyes—raw and unspoken. "I'm not here to babysit," he said quietly, dropping his voice as though sharing a dangerous secret. "I'm here to make sure you stay alive. Whether you like it or not."

Silence fell between them—a thick, suffocating weight. The faint ticking of the clock on the wall punctuated the stillness like a slow heartbeat. Elena searched his face, hunting for any hint of weakness, some subtle crack in the impenetrable mask. There was nothing. Just steady, unyielding resolve.

For a brief heartbeat, she allowed herself to feel it—the magnetic pull that made her lean forward even as every instinct screamed to pull away.

"Fine," she said at last, voice steady but the words tasting bitter, like ash on her tongue. "But stay out of my way."

A flicker of a smile curved his lips—amused, unreadable— and it stirred an unexpected irritation in her, sharper than she anticipated.

"Understood," he replied smoothly. But beneath the calm surface lurked something else—something that unsettled her. Something that whispered staying out of her way would be the hardest thing he'd ever do.

Elena didn't need him—not really. But watching him stand there, unwavering and unflinching, she knew one thing for sure: he wasn't going anywhere.

Chapter 2: Danger at Every Turn

Elena lingered in the dim briefing room long after Logan had left, her fingers resting hesitantly on the folder he'd placed on the table. Its weight was tangible in her hands, as if the contents inside mirrored the heavy burden she carried— threats mounting, alliances fracturing, and a shadow that stretched further than she dared admit. Her frustration simmered beneath the surface, tangled with a restless unease she couldn't shake.

The day stretched out in endless succession of meetings and policy briefings, each one blurring into the next beneath the Capitol's soaring ceilings. But beneath the polished pronouncements and political posturing, the earlier phone call gnawed at her—a sharp, persistent splinter lodged deep in her mind. Every distorted syllable of that chilling ultimatum echoed relentlessly, threading through her nerves like ice narrowing her chest. It wasn't merely the threat itself—it was the way it undermined her, made her feel small and exposed in a world she'd long commanded with unyielding confidence. She despised the cracks it revealed— the doubt, the vulnerability creeping in around the edges of her armor.

Logan's presence hovered nearby throughout it all—an almost constant shadow at the edges of her awareness. He positioned himself with the careful precision of a predator— close enough to be protective, but never intrusive. His steady gaze traced her movements with quiet intensity, and the deliberate calm in his every gesture sent a jolt of tension skittering across her skin. It unnerved her, this hyperawareness of being watched, weighed, and measured even in a crowded room. And yet, beneath the flare of irritation, an unwelcome thread of comfort wove through her resistance—a quiet promise nestled in his unwavering vigilance that unsettled her more than she cared to admit.

There was something about the way Logan moved—certain, controlled, almost unyielding—that rattled her deep down. It was as if he could see beyond the poised congresswoman, past the carefully constructed façades, all the way to the woman beneath—the one who hated how much she noticed him: the way he didn't miss a single detail, the subtle sharpness in his eyes, and how they somehow always found her, no matter the distraction.

By the time she finally pushed through the Capitol's heavy doors, the evening air had turned biting cold, slicing through the layers of her coat. She instinctively pulled it tighter around her, her mind still a tempest of looming threats, intricate strategies, and the persistent gravity of the man who matched her step for step.

"Car's this way," Logan's voice dropped low as he appeared beside her. It was professional, but underneath simmered an indefinable current—something she couldn't quite place. His hand hovered close to the small of her back—never touching, but close enough that the warmth of his proximity seeped through the fabric. The subtle gesture ignited an unexpected heat within her, and she loathed the betrayal of that instinctive reaction, the silent admission it forced upon her.

As they approached the waiting vehicle, Logan's entire posture shifted. His head snapped toward the darkened street, sharp eyes scanning with a hunter's precision. The tension coiled taut in him like a spring ready to snap. Elena's stomach clenched reflexively, and a shiver raced down her spine. Without thinking, she stepped closer, drawn to the silent strength he radiated, even as she wrestled with the unease it stirred.

"Get in. Now." His voice was low, cold, and absolute—leaving no room for hesitation.

"What—" Elena began, but Logan cut her off.

"Now," he repeated firmly, opening the door and practically ushering her inside. His movements were swift, but precise—controlled. She barely had time to register the urgency before he slid in right after her. "Driver, move."

The SUV surged into traffic. City lights blurred and smeared across the tinted windows as the vehicle sped away, the deep hum of the engine filling the uneasy silence. The confined space felt charged, taut with unspoken tension.

"What's happening?" Elena demanded, her voice tight, heart pounding in her chest.

Logan pressed a hand to his earpiece without hesitation. "We've got a tail. Dark sedan, four o'clock. Likely Donovan's men, but I can't confirm weaponry yet."

Her breath caught sharply, a cold spike racing through her veins. "Are they armed?"

"Probably," Logan replied, calm to a fault. His measured steadiness grated against her nerves, a sharp contrast to the storm swirling in her mind. How did he manage to stay so composed while she felt like she was unraveling? The disparity unnerved her—like he could peer through the polished exterior she worked so hard to maintain and see the fragile fissures beneath. That thought left her feeling exposed, raw. But that wasn't her priority now—not when the threat was real and closing in.

"I'm not about to give them the chance, either," Logan said quietly, eyes fixed ahead on the road and the threat lurking behind.

The driver cut sharply into a narrow alley, tires skimming over loose gravel. Elena braced herself against the seat, a surge of adrenaline making her muscles tense. She cast a quick glance at Logan — jaw tight, brows furrowed — his entire body coiled with alertness as he tracked the sedan's pursuit. There was something magnetic about his focus: a blend of raw control and fierce determination that set her pulse racing for reasons she struggled to name.

As the SUV veered back onto a wider street, the sedan finally pulled away into the darkness, its taillights vanishing like a shadow swallowed by the night. The immediate danger had passed, but the charged tension lingered, thick and suffocating.

Logan's hand dropped from the earpiece. "We're clear—for now."

Elena exhaled slowly, but her chest remained tight, her limbs still humming with unease. "This is my life now?" she murmured, more to herself than anyone else.

"Only as long as you keep going after Donovan," Logan said bluntly. His words landed with hard certainty, slicing through the moment with undeniable truth.

Giving up was never an option. Fear didn't get to dictate her path. Yet, sitting beside him in the dim glow of the SUV's interior, she couldn't deny the odd comfort his presence offered—a tether in the swirling chaos.

The ride to her townhouse unfolded in near silence, broken only by the faint crackling of Logan's radio scanning for threats. Elena's mind churned — replaying the day's events, the ominous calls, the escape, the man beside her. She despised feeling out of control. His quiet authority only made her more aware of every shallow breath, every subtle movement between them.

Despite the danger and uncertainty, Logan's steady presence grounded her in an unexpected way — a complicated calm she both resisted and desperately needed.

Elena kept her eyes fixed on the dark ribbon of road ahead, though her thoughts tangled into a restless whirlpool she couldn't quite grasp. Independence had always been her anchor—relying on anyone was a foreign notion. Yet Logan Chase, her so-called protector, unraveled that certainty thread by thread. He sat beside her, unmoving but alert, eyes scanning their surroundings with professional precision. And still, beneath that calm exterior, she felt it—a silent current of tension, tightly coiled, impossible to shake.

She couldn't decide if his stoicism grated her nerves or quietly drew her in. Maybe it was both. It wasn't just the fact that he was striking—though she wouldn't deny the flicker of attraction sparked every time his gaze lingered longer than necessary. It was something deeper, more unsettling: the way he absorbed everything without complaint, his quiet confidence settling over the space like a shadow she couldn't outrun. It made her skin crawl—that feeling of exposure, as if he saw straight through the armor she'd painstakingly constructed.

The SUV finally eased to a stop. Logan was the first to move, slipping out of the car and wordlessly opening her door. Elena followed, her pulse quickening with a charge she refused to analyze or admit—even to herself. His voice broke the silence, rough and commanding, drawing a sharp line in the air between them.

"Stay close."

As she stepped out, his hand brushed briefly against her arm—fleeting, almost accidental—and yet the jolt it sent racing through her veins flared like a warning flare. She clenched her fists, willing the strange heat to fade. He couldn't be a distraction. She wouldn't let him be.

Inside the warmth of her townhouse, vanilla softened the air, a small comfort against the cold outside. She shrugged off her coat, letting it fall carelessly over a chair, and turned to find Logan already surveying the room with a hawk's eye. His stance was rigid, posture primed by the door. The man didn't know how to relax, the distance he maintained as much a safeguard for himself as it was his professional shield.

"Everything looks secure," he reported, voice clipped and exact, a declaration rather than a conversation.

"Good." Her tone sliced sharper than she intended—a blade forged from frustration and something rawer, more vulnerable. She didn't want him here. She didn't want to admit how much his presence frayed the edges of her carefully maintained control. "You can go now."

Logan's eyes narrowed minutely, but he didn't move. "I'll stay tonight. Just to be safe."

She crossed her arms, holding his gaze with a challenge sharpened by unease. "That's not necessary."

His words came like a strike, final and unyielding. "It's not up for debate." The cold steel in his eyes twisted something deep inside her—stirring resistance and something dangerously close to longing. She hated orders, especially from him. And yet, a part of her hesitated—the part that didn't feel unsafe with him near, but oddly anchored.

The silence stretched taut between them, heavy and electric, until she finally exhaled sharply and ran a hand through her hair, seeking composure in the chaos. "Fine. Suit yourself."

The words tasted bitter in her mouth, thick with frustration and something unnamed—an uncomfortable blend of resentment and reluctant acceptance. Part of her wanted to argue, to push back harder, to prove she didn't need protection. But another, quieter part—one she refused to name—welcomed it. She was used to solitude, to control. Yet with him here, a magnetic pull tugged at the edges of her resolve, a tangled knot of emotion she wasn't ready to face.

She turned abruptly away, breaking the charged eye contact, stifling the urge to speak more—fearing what might spill out if she didn't.

Elena moved into the kitchen, seeking space to breathe, craving a momentary escape from the suffocating closeness of Logan's presence. He didn't follow, but she could almost feel his gaze tracing her every movement, an invisible weight pressing down in the small townhouse. It suddenly felt smaller, tighter, as if he occupied more space than the walls allowed—his presence a silent claim on her territory.

Later that evening, the air thickened with an unspoken tension, coiling tighter between them like a storm gathering on the horizon. Elena curled into the familiar curve of the couch, her fingers wrapped loosely around a wineglass, warmth blossoming inside her chest and limbs. The soft glow from the lamp cast flickering shadows across the room as her gaze drifted upward—landing on Logan standing framed by the doorway. He commanded the space effortlessly, his silhouette broad and still, demanding attention without a single word. Fueled by the wine and the magnetic pull of his nearness, she let her eyes roam over him slowly, feeling a reckless emboldenment beneath her skin.

"You should get some rest," his voice broke the silence— soft but firm, edged with a quiet authority that made the space between them pulse.

Elena smirked, swirling the deep red liquid in her glass, watching how the dim light caught in its depths. "I could say the same to you," she teased, voice low. "Do you ever relax?"

A flicker—barely perceptible—tugged at the corner of his lips, but his eyes remained cool and unreadable. "Not when I'm on the job."

"Oh." She arched a brow, amusement dancing in her eyes. "So, you just want me out of the way?"

Logan's gaze sharpened, a spark igniting deep within their locked stare. "No. It's not like that. I want you well-rested."

She set down the glass with deliberate calm and rose, moving toward him before the caution inside her could catch up. The pull was irresistible—a magnetic force twisting tighter with every breath. "You need to rest too," she said, voice lower now, laced with an unexpected softness. "You deserve to relax. You can't always be... so tense. So on guard."

His eyes darkened, shadows flickering in their depths as he took a measured step back, as if creating distance both physically and emotionally. "I have to be. Especially around you."

Elena closed the space between them by another slow step, reckless and deliberate. "That sounds exhausting." She tilted her head, watching his every reaction—a predator's patience mingled with something almost fragile. "No distractions. No indulgences…" Her voice dropped to a whisper, the air contracting between them. "No fun."

His jaw clenched, but his fierce gaze never wavered. "I don't need distractions."

She let out a soft, knowing hum, the edge of a smile playing on her lips. "That doesn't mean you don't want them, does it?"

His hesitation twisted something deep in her stomach—a tight knot of unease and curiosity.

"But you're—" she began, only to watch him cut himself off, shaking his head as if to banish the unspoken thought. "It doesn't matter."

She arched a brow, voice low and teasing. "Do you think I'm dangerous?"

Logan's involuntary step back answered before he did.

A slow, deliberate smile curved her lips, like a cat savoring the chase. "Maybe I should be the one keeping my guard up."

He exhaled sharply through his nose—a sound somewhere between a laugh and a growl—but the fire in his eyes was anything but amused. "You don't know what you're doing."

"Don't I?" She reached out, letting a single fingertip trace lightly down the sleeve of his shirt—fragile, teasing, just enough to gauge his nerve. She felt him tense beneath her touch, coiled taut like a spring ready to snap.

"I think you just don't like that I see through you." Her voice dropped, layered with challenge and something darker, more vulnerable.

His breath grew heavier, chest rising and falling as if he were restraining himself from breaking free.

"Elena." The word came low, barely a whisper—a plea buried beneath steel.

She tilted her head, studying the lines of his face, searching for the walls he tried so hard to keep up. "What are you so afraid of?"

For a flicker of a heartbeat, something raw and volatile flared in his expression—heat, want, restraint straining to hold its ground. She thought he might close the distance, might shatter the fragile tension — but then a muscle twitched in his jaw, and he stepped back, forcing control back over the storm.

"This isn't personal," he ground out, voice rough with conflict. "It can't be."

And yet—the way his gaze drifted downward to her lips, the hitch in his breath as she leaned in ever so slightly—said exactly the opposite.

Elena let the silence linger, thick and electric, savoring the raw power in the space between them. She could push further—one step more, one touch deeper—and watch him break apart.

But he moved first.

"Get some rest," Logan said, voice clipped, as if the moment had never happened. "I'll be here if you need me."

Then he was gone, leaving her alone in the dim room, heart hammering, breath shallow.

She watched the shadow he left behind, an ache settling deep beneath her ribs—frustration, longing, and something unspoken. She couldn't stop picturing the way his face had closed off just before he turned away, as if locking away a secret she wasn't sure she wanted unearthed. Maybe it was better that way.

Her hand rose to her forehead, pressing firmly as if to steady the dizzy rush of emotions swirling inside her. The wine had loosened her guard too much—let her slip in ways she rarely permitted. Control was her currency, her weapon; she wasn't the kind of woman who faltered or let a man like Logan unravel her.

But with him—the rules seemed to evaporate.

The real danger wasn't just the threats stalking her from the shadows, the anonymous calls that promised ruin. No—danger lived in the way Logan unsettled her so completely, stripped away years of armor with a single look, a single touch.

Trust, vulnerability, the simmering tension twisted between them—it was a storm far more treacherous than any enemy waiting in the dark.

And beneath it all, an undeniable pulse thrummed—raw and unyielding.

For the first time in a long time, Elena wasn't in control.

And that terrified her.

Chapter 3: Beneath the Surface

The faint, pale glow of dawn filtered through the heavy curtains of Elena's townhouse, casting long, fragile shadows that stretched lazily across the quiet room. She stood motionless by the window, her gaze fixed on the empty street below, though she saw little of it. Outside, the city was waking, the first stirrings of a new day whispering through distant sounds—the muted hum of a lone car engine, the soft trill of a waking bird—but instead of comfort, these familiar noises unsettled her. It was as if the world was awakening to something she wasn't ready to face, a looming shift too large to ignore. The weight of the day pressed down on her chest, heavy and unrelenting, the knowledge coiling tightly inside: everything was about to change.

Before she could turn, she sensed him—Logan's presence was a constant shadow at her side, an unyielding reminder of the danger she couldn't outrun. She heard his footsteps first, quiet and measured on the floor, followed by the subtle shift in his posture as he scanned the dim street below. He was always watching, always alert, as if every shadow held a threat only he could detect. Yet despite his rigid control, the stillness in his stance grated on her nerves. She hated that she needed him, that he was the one tasked with keeping her safe. But he was—whether she wanted to admit it or not.

"We need to head to the Capitol," Elena said, breaking the heavy silence. She stepped further into the room, the sharp precision of her tailored navy suit catching the growing light, her heels clicking softly against the hardwood floor. Her posture was flawless, but the tension nestled in her shoulders and the tight line of her mouth betrayed the storm swirling beneath her composed exterior. She knew Logan would see it—the faint flicker of hesitation in her eyes, the cracks in her otherwise unshakeable resolve. She couldn't afford to let him see more.

"I have a meeting in two hours that I can't miss," she added, voice controlled though underscored by an undeniable edge of uncertainty. It was partly true—attendance was important—but it wasn't the full truth. There were other reasons she couldn't stay hidden. She refused to be cowed by Donovan's threats. She would face whatever came.

Logan's gaze sharpened as he turned to face her. His eyes narrowed slightly, jaw tightening in a silent battle between the need to protect and the respect for her stubbornness. She caught the faintest trace of concern he fought to bury. She didn't need his worry. She didn't want his interference. She had navigated these perilous waters for years without an escort. She wouldn't start now.

"It's not safe," Logan said flatly, frustration threading his tone.

Crossing her arms firmly, Elena felt the fiery stubbornness flare within. She met his gaze with unwavering defiance, every muscle tense with resolve. "I don't have a choice," she said. "Donovan's threats won't push me into hiding."

The silence between them thickened, loaded with unspoken words. Logan's eyes hardened, the unreadable set of his expression reflecting the conflict gnawing at him. She could see the protector in him warring with the man who knew her will wasn't easily broken. Understanding wasn't what she sought from him. She didn't expect it. But she knew, deep down, he understood anyway.

Finally, he nodded, the reluctant consent etched in the tight line of his jaw and the slight tension in his shoulders. "Fine," he said tersely. "But we take my route. And you stick close to me. No exceptions."

Elena said nothing, but the heavy grip tightening her chest loosened just a fraction. She wasn't sure why she agreed— not because she trusted him fully, but because in that moment, she knew he wouldn't let her face the fight alone. And somehow, that knowledge offered a flicker of unexpected relief—fragile, yet present.

***

The ride to the Capitol blurred outward in muted grays and dull shapes as Elena sat rigid beside Logan, her hands clasped tightly in her lap. Her gaze drifted past the window, but she barely saw the world slipping by—a ghost of movement and color that seemed distant, unreal compared to the sharp stillness inside the car. The low hum of the engine filled the small space, punctuated only by the silence that enveloped them like a tightening noose.

Logan's presence was magnetic, even in the quiet. She couldn't help but notice how every inch of his body was taut with focus. His hands gripped the wheel with deliberate control, eyes flicking constantly between the road ahead and the rearview mirror, each movement precise and purposeful. It wasn't just vigilance—it was a primal readiness, an unyielding calculation that radiated through the vehicle like a living thing.

The weight of that control pressed down on her. Elena's throat tightened with an urge to speak, to break the silence with something—anything—but the moment never felt quite right. Every time she opened her mouth, the fragile equilibrium of Logan's carefully maintained calm threatened to fracture. So she remained silent, each passing second making the quiet feel heavier, more suffocating.

As they neared the secured parking beneath the Capitol, Elena caught the subtle shift in Logan's posture—an almost imperceptible tightening of his muscles, a sharper focus in his narrowed eyes as they scanned their surroundings. She followed the line of his gaze instinctively, but saw nothing unusual—only the familiar throng of government workers hastening through their routines, visitors weaving through the stone columns. Still, she knew better than to doubt the vigilance carved into his every movement.

"Elena," his voice came low, steady, slicing through the stillness like a blade. "This is routine. But keep your head down when we exit. I'll guide you."

She didn't argue. In that rare, quiet moment, the usual fire within her flickered into stillness. It wasn't surrender—far from it. The authority in his tone was something she recognized, deeply instinctual. She wanted to trust it, to lean into the security it promised. For the first time that day, the small thread of calm that Logan wove around her felt like a fragile lifeline—unexpected, but necessary.

***

The morning blurred into an unrelenting stream of meetings and briefings, each one a gauntlet she had to navigate with sharpened focus. Skeptical committee members scrutinized her words, probing reporters lurked at the edges, and Donovan's long shadow stretched like a threat over every conversation. But with every challenge, her resolve coiled tighter, forged harder. She spoke with precision and cold confidence, her arguments slicing through doubt like a razor—unyielding, unswayed. Yet beneath the veneer of control, she couldn't shake the persistent awareness: Logan was always there.

Silent. Watchful. Unblinking.

It wasn't just the closeness of his presence that unsettled her, but the weight behind his gaze whenever their eyes brushed. In those moments, it felt like he was searching for something beneath the polished mask she wore—a part of her she rarely let anyone see. Her pulse would quicken uncontrollably, a subtle tremor she struggled to name. It wasn't purely protection; it was something darker, more complex. He wasn't just guarding her body—he was watching her soul.

When the final meeting ended and the afternoon sun hung low, casting long, jagged shadows through the Capitol's soaring corridors, the full weight of the day crashed over her. Exhaustion nestled against her bones, heavy and insistent. She retreated to the quiet sanctuary of her office, sinking into the worn leather chair as Valerie approached with tomorrow's agenda. The paper felt heavier in her hands, the worries multiplying beneath the polished surface of her professionalism.

"That's enough for today," Elena said, her voice firmer than she'd felt moments ago, an attempt to command the weariness to retreat. "Thanks, Val. Get some rest."

Valerie hesitated, a small, understanding smile flickering before she nodded and slipped through the door.

Elena's gaze shifted across the room to Logan, who had settled into a chair nearby. Though his posture was more relaxed than earlier, there was still a steeliness beneath the calm—the watchful precision of a man never fully at ease. But the silence between them no longer felt like a gauntlet. For the first time that day, it held a fragile reprieve, a momentary truce from the day's relentless pressure.

"You didn't have to sit through all that," Elena murmured, her voice softer than she intended, fatigue loosening her usual guarded edges.

Logan arched a brow, lips twitching with a subtle smirk. "I'm here to keep you safe. That includes enduring boring committee meetings."

A genuine laugh escaped her—sharp, unexpected, and light. They both seemed surprised by the momentary lift. "Boring? I thought appropriations debates would have you captivated."

His smirk deepened, the corners of his mouth tugging with amused resignation. "Riveting, truly."

For a fleeting second, the walls around them softened, and the air warmed with unsaid camaraderie. But the weight of their reality settled swiftly back into the room like an unwanted guest.

"Donovan isn't going to back down," Elena said quietly, voice leveling with steel and unswerving determination despite the fatigue clinging to her muscles. "And today proved just how much I won't either."

Logan's gaze sharpened, locking onto hers with a gravity that mirrored her own fierce resolve. "Good," he said, voice low and steady. "Because giving up is not an option."

In that suspended moment, Elena felt it—clear and undeniable—that despite every shadow and threat, she wasn't fighting this battle alone.

***

The Capitol's labyrinthine corridors stretched before her— dim, shadowed, unnervingly silent. Elena's pace quickened intentionally, staying close to Logan, matching each deliberate, controlled step he took. His hand hovered near the concealed holster beneath his jacket, a taut promise of protection that only tightened the coil of nerves constricting her chest. The faint echo of their shoes clicked loudly against the polished marble, slicing through the stillness and heightening the oppressive quiet.

"How much farther?" she whispered, her voice fragile, as if louder words might shatter the fragile calm.

Logan's reply was clipped, edged with relentless focus. "We're headed to a secure exit. Stay close. Keep quiet."

Before Elena could respond, the silence shattered—metallic and sharp—a distant door slammed shut. Her heart jumped, the suddenness igniting panic. Logan froze instantly, body rigid, every muscle honed for action. He raised a hand in a sharp stop signal.

Pulse hammering in her ears, Elena barely breathed out, "What is it?"

Without looking back, Logan's tone dropped to a low command: "Wait here." Then he flowed forward—steps soundless yet sure, a shadow slipping into the dark.

Elena remained rooted; her limbs taut as bowstrings. Each shallow breath stabbed at her lungs, time stretching and twisting until the sudden crash echoed through the corridor—a violent eruption followed by a sharp, anguished yell. Panic surged, a wild tide threatening to drown her. She wanted to move, to follow—but Logan's silent return stopped her.

"We've got company. Move!" His grip on her hand was firm but measured, grounding her chaos without crushing it.

They bolted, feet pounding crystal against marble, echoes relentless as muffled shouts and the thunder of boots grew closer behind them. The air thickened, pressing in with urgency and fear.

Logan veered sharply into a shadowed alcove, yanking open a hidden door. "Inside!" he barked, pulling her through just as the heavy door clicked shut, muffling the frenetic sounds of pursuit.

The cramped space closed in, cooler and stifling, the air still but heavy. Logan pressed his ear to the wall, breathing steady despite the storm outside. Elena pressed her back against the cold stone, trying to harness her ragged breaths, her chest tight with rushing adrenaline. Thoughts scrambled; clarity elusive.

Her voice barely above a breath, she asked, "What now?"

Logan turned, eyes sharp in the dim light, and pointed toward a narrow stairwell descending into shadow. "This leads to the underground lot. We'll take my car. The townhouse is secure."

The weight of his words sank in, moment crystallizing with sudden gravity. Uncertainty tugged at her resolve. "And if they follow us?"

His voice was steady, unwavering, a final promise. "They won't. Move."

***

As they navigated the tangled city streets, the air inside the car grew heavy—thick and charged with an unspoken weight. The steady hum of the engine was the only sound, a low drone that filled the silence but never quite pierced it. The space between them felt taut, stretched thin like a fragile thread ready to snap.

Elena's eyes flicked toward Logan, catching the subtle lines of concentration etched on his face in the dim interior light. Beneath his focused calm, she sensed something deeper—an unspoken presence anchoring her in the swirling chaos outside the vehicle. It was more than protection. It was a quiet constancy that reached into the spaces she usually kept locked tight.

For the first time, awareness bloomed within her: she trusted him. Not just with her life, but with everything she usually guarded so fiercely. The realization hit like a sudden chill, sharp and unwelcome, stealing the breath from her lungs. That kind of trust was unfamiliar territory—a dangerous vulnerability she wasn't prepared to own.

She didn't want to acknowledge it, to lay bare the fragile threads binding them. Still, the truth settled deep in her bones, pulsing beneath the surface like a secret heartbeat. And that—more than any threat Donovan had cast—terrified her.

Chapter 4: Tangled Webs

Elena's footsteps echoed softly against the hardwood floor of her townhouse, each pace slow and deliberate as shadows lengthened and curled like dark fingers along the walls. Outside the tall windows, Logan remained—a still silhouette beneath the pale flicker of streetlamps, watching as though guarding more than just her home. Earlier, his hand had pressed against her arm, firm yet gentle; the imprint lingered, a silent reminder of the boundary she both needed and resented.

Her laptop lay open on the glass coffee table, a chaotic constellation of files and fragmented emails spread in disarray. Somewhere hidden within that digital labyrinth was the evidence she desperately sought—proof to expose Donovan's carefully veiled corruption. But fatigue draped itself over her like a heavy cloak, pulling at her limbs as she sank onto the couch, though her mind raced with restless urgency.

The soft click of the front door disrupted the thickening silence. Logan stepped inside, his presence slicing through the tension. "Still pacing," he observed, voice low, threaded with concern.

Elena closed her eyes for a moment, pressing her fingers against her temple in a vain attempt to ease the pounding thoughts. "I can't stop. Donovan's behind every threat, but without something solid—financial transactions, emails, anything linking him directly—it's just shadows." Her hand swept across the mess on the table, frustration simmering beneath her calm exterior. "He's meticulous. It's like hunting a ghost."

Leaning against the doorframe, Logan's gaze was steady but softened with an unspoken warning. "You don't have to carry this burden alone."

She swallowed hard, the old ache of isolation twisting her insides. "Why do you care? Why risk yourself for this?"

His answer came without hesitation, quiet but steady: "Because I've seen what men like Donovan are willing to sacrifice to stay buried, and I won't stand by and watch you become one of the casualties."

The weight of his sincerity crept past her armor, cracking something fragile within. Weeks of solitary struggle had begun to erode her confidence—yet here was someone, offering a shield when she felt most exposed. Her voice trembled with vulnerability. "I really don't have space for distractions."

Logan's expression held firm. "This isn't one."

Suddenly, her phone vibrated sharply against the table. She glanced down—an urgent message: Check your email. Now. Heart thudding, she reopened her laptop. An encrypted file sat waiting, anonymous but unmistakable—offshore accounts, illicit contracts, a thread unraveling Donovan's web.

"This might be the break we need," she breathed, fingers dancing across the keyboard.

Logan stepped closer, merging with the shadows behind her. "Trust the source?"

Elena hesitated; the danger palpable. "I don't. But it's a risk worth taking."

A sudden crash shattered the fragile calm. Logan was at the window before she could react, gun drawn, senses razor-sharp. "Stay inside," he commanded, slipping silently into the night.

Elena's breath hitched, ears straining against the thickening silence. Voices, muffled at first, grew sharp—a single gunshot cracked the stillness. Panic seized her chest. She flung open the door to find Logan looming over a man sprawled unconscious on the stoop, weapon still raised.

"Nothing more than a lackey," Logan muttered, pulling her back inside. "They're probing, testing our defenses."

Her knees felt weak, the reality sinking in. "They won't stop until we do."

His grip on her arm tightened, steadying. "Exactly. And we will." This sounds like they are going to stop. Doesn't make sense to me.

For the first time in weeks, a tentative light stirred within Elena—hope, fragile but fierce. Her eyes sought Logan's, and despite everything, she dared to believe.

***

Elena stood near the window, arms crossed tightly against her chest as if trying to hold herself together in the thick, charged air that clung to the room like fog. The aftermath of the confrontation weighed on every surface—the faint smell of sweat and adrenaline mingled with the stale scent of spent gunpowder and dust. Outside, the doorstep where the struggle had briefly unfolded was now eerily quiet.

Logan's voice broke the silence, sharp and controlled as he brought his phone to his ear. "This is Logan Chase," he said, steady but clipped. "We've got a hostile down at the Capitol Hill townhouse. Request immediate containment."

Elena's ears strained to catch the reply—something about the FBI being en route, instructions to hold tight. His eyes flicked to her, unreadable in the dim light, but his posture was taut with alertness.

When he ended the call, Logan faced her fully. "FBIs on their way, but they'll secure the scene first. We can't stick around long."

A tight knot swelled in Elena's chest, twisting with a mix of fear and urgency. "It's spiraling faster than I imagined," she admitted in a low voice, voice barely above a whisper. "What if… what if it all falls apart? What if we don't make it through this?"

Logan stepped forward, closing the distance between them with purposeful calm. His eyes were steady, anchoring her turbulent thoughts. "We will. I promise you; I won't let anything happen to you."

Before she could find the words to respond, the wailing shriek of sirens tore through the early evening air. Within moments, a team of FBI agents flooded into the townhouse—movements precise and practiced, filling the space with urgent authority.

A tall woman with sharp, no-nonsense features approached them, voice brisk and businesslike. "Congresswoman Delgado. Logan Chase. I'm Agent Parker. The perimeter's secure, but this isn't over. Donovan's reach is deep. If he learns you're still alive, you're targets—both of you."

Elena swallowed hard, the weight of Parker's words sinking in like ice water down her spine. "Disappear? I'm a sitting member of Congress. Vanishing isn't exactly… feasible."

Parker's expression softened just enough to betray the burden beneath her professionalism. "Your safety takes priority. We'll handle the public story. But you and Mr. Chase need to go dark—for now—until we can gather irrefutable evidence to bring Donovan down."

Logan accepted a sealed envelope from Parker, peeling back the security tape. "New identities, secure transport, communication channels—everything we'll need."

"There's a safe house about fifty miles outside the city," Parker explained. "Regroup there and lay low."

The bustling agents moved methodically, processing the scene while Logan guided Elena toward a quieter corner, away from prying ears. Her hands trembled—just slightly—but enough to betray the storm inside. Her breath hitched as she fought to steady herself.

"Hey," Logan's voice softened as his fingers brushed along her arm—not with force, but reassurance. "We'll figure this out. Together."

She met his gaze, vulnerability and fierce resolve warring in her eyes. "This isn't just about me. Donovan's corruption is poison—destroying lives far beyond this room."

"I know," Logan replied, voice low but unwavering. "That's exactly why we stop him. But first, survival."

Elena exhaled slowly, swallowing the panic to find focus. "So… what's the plan?"

"Lay low," Logan said, jaw set with determination. "Disappear for a while, but no sitting on our hands. We'll dig deep—follow the money, expose the lies."

The quiet flame of determination flickered and grew in her eyes, solid and unshakeable. "If we do this, it's together. I'm not running while you bear the risk alone."

A faint, knowing smile tugged at Logan's lips—a rare crack in his usually guarded demeanor. "Wouldn't expect anything less."

His words hung between them, heavy with urgency and unspoken promises. There wasn't time to linger; he gave a curt nod.

"Let's move. The sooner we're out, the better."

As they stepped outside into the chill night under the watchful eyes of the FBI, Elena's gaze lingered on Logan. Despite the chaos swirling around them, he felt like a steady anchor in a storm—solid, reliable, someone she could trust. Completely.

Chapter 5: Close Quarters

The quiet charm of Virginia's countryside unfolded around them as the SUV wound through gentle rolling hills. Middleburg appeared like a scene preserved from another era: cobblestone streets bordered by historic brick buildings, their warm reds and browns glowing beneath a canopy of vibrant autumn leaves. The calm beauty felt surreal—an uneasy balm against the chaos Elena and Logan had left behind.

Elena pressed her forehead to the cool glass of the window, the crisp air outside seeming worlds away. Thoughts knotted in her mind—fear tangled with stubborn resolve. The weight of their flight pressed on her chest, but it was Logan she found hardest to hold at bay. Not just as her protector anymore, but as something dangerously intimate.

The crunch of gravel beneath tires pulled her back. The SUV slowed near a small clearing, nestled among towering pines that swayed softly in the evening breeze. Logan moved first, stepping out with the practiced vigilance of someone who never let down his guard. He scanned the grove with sharp eyes before reaching for her door.

"It's not much," he said, voice low but steady, "but it'll keep us safe."

Elena slipped out, hugging herself against the sharp bite of the cool air. The scent of damp earth and pine needles wrapped around her—a quiet contrast to the sterile, oppressive confines of the city. Crickets trilled softly nearby, their steady cadence emphasizing the stillness settling in the woods.

She inhaled deeply. "It's perfect," she said, eyes lingering on the modest cabin where a fire flickered warmly in the hearth. "Thank you."

Logan crossed to the cabin's entrance, moving with a soldier's efficiency—checking doors, peering out windows, muscles tensed for threats unseen. Elena watched him, her own nerves taut, heart thrumming with a mix of exhaustion and adrenaline. The weight of everything bearing down on her felt heavier here, despite the serenity.

Finally, Logan turned toward her. His expression softened for the first time in hours. "We're secure. You should rest. Tomorrow, we start planning."

She hesitated; voice small. "Logan... thank you. I don't know how I'd get through this without you."

She was drawn to him, the way some people are drawn to flames even knowing they start fires.

She drifted into the small kitchen, her eyes briefly taking in the sparse supplies with a wry, knowing glance. "If we're going to hide out," she murmured, a faint, almost mischievous smile curling the corners of her lips, "we should at least eat well."

Logan's mouth twitched at the corner, nearly a smile. "You cook?"

"I survive," she shot back, pulling a box of pasta and a jar of rich tomato sauce from the pantry with casual confidence.

Within minutes, they fell into an easy, unspoken rhythm. Logan chopped vegetables with military precision—the crisp knife strokes sharp and methodical—while she stirred the sauce gently, sneaking quick glances in his direction when she thought he wasn't looking. The kitchen air grew warm and inviting, filled with the mingling scents of garlic, herbs, and faint woodsmoke wafting in from the stone hearth. Yet it wasn't just the food that made her chest tighten—it was the nearness of him. Their sleeves brushed once, twice, sparking a silent current of awareness neither tried to dismiss.

By the time they sat down at the small, worn table to eat, the earlier tension had softened into playful banter about who deserved the title of better cook. Each quip, light yet charged, drew them closer, threading an intimacy that words alone couldn't convey. When she poured them each a glass of deep red wine, Logan lifted a brow in mock warning.

"Careful," he said, his voice low and teasing, "loose lips sink ships."

Her smile deepened, and she leaned just a fraction nearer, her eyes locking with his. "And sometimes," she whispered back, letting the words hang like a spark in the warm kitchen light, "they start fires."

The moment stretched between them—charged, fragile, and filled with possibilities unspoken but understood.

The words settled deep inside her, loosening a tension she hadn't realized had fastened itself around her ribs. The space between them shrank, charged with an unspoken pull—one she had tried to ignore.

Her breath caught as Logan reached up, fingers brushing a loose strand of hair from her face. The touch was light, tentative but electric, sending a shiver she couldn't suppress down her spine.

"Logan…" she whispered, voice trembling under the weight of everything left unsaid.

For a breathless moment, he seemed poised to speak, but his silence said more—his gaze locked on hers, raw and unguarded. Elena's own resolve wavered; fear and hope warred within her.

Her voice cracked the stillness, fragile but honest. "I…"

The words died on her lips, swallowed by the moment. Instead, she let herself reach out, closing the distance between them in a sudden, desperate kiss—tender and fierce all at once. Logan blinked, surprised, then yielded willingly.

His arms wrapped around her, firm and grounding, pulling her close. Her hands traced along his broad chest, memorizing the solid weight beneath her fingers as desire flickered dangerously to the surface. The kiss deepened, a fusion of longing and release, as if the suffocating tension and swirling chaos could dissolve in this fragile connection.

When they finally parted, breathless and trembling, Elena rested her forehead against his, eyes fluttering open to meet his intense gaze. "I needed that," she confessed, voice rough with emotion. "I needed you."

Logan's usual stoicism softened, revealing something vulnerable beneath. "I'm here," he murmured, "and I'm not going anywhere."

Her fingers traced along the sharp line of his jaw, lingering on the rough stubble beneath her touch. "You've always been so careful, so guarded," she said, voice barely above a whisper. "But I can feel it —the connection between us. Have you? All this time?"

He finally answered with a quiet smile edged with bittersweet honesty. "I've tried to keep my distance. But from the moment we met, it's been a battle I couldn't win."

Elena's heart fluttered, courage sparking new warmth within her. "Then stop fighting," she said, voice steady as her fingers slid into the thick strands of his hair. "I don't want you holding back—not from me."

Logan's hands tightened around her waist, the restraint he'd held for so long thinning like fragile paper catching flame. His voice, rough with vulnerability, broke the heavy silence. "Are you sure, Elena?"

A slow, confident smile curved her lips, a mischievous glint sparkling in her eyes. "I've never been surer," she said, her hands sliding down to rest lightly but deliberately on his hips. "I want to explore this connection—every part of it. Starting right now."

Her touch was both an invitation and a promise as she guided him toward the worn leather sofa. The quiet crackle of the low-burning fire filled the room, casting flickering shadows that danced over their faces, warming the cool air between them. As they moved, Elena's fingers deftly flicked open the buttons of his shirt, the soft fabric slipping away to reveal a sculpted torso taut with muscle. Underneath her touch, Logan's breath hitched, each ripple of muscle a silent testament to the years he'd spent keeping danger at bay— and now surrendering, piece by piece.

They sank down onto the sofa, the cushions creaking softly beneath their weight. Elena settled over his waist, eyes locked with his in a charged gaze that held both challenge and tenderness. Her lips met his again—a kiss hungry and demanding, tongues tracing a fiery dance that spoke of buried longing and newfound courage.

Her hands roamed boldly, her palms and fingertips mapping the broad expanse of his chest and the hard plane of his abdomen, before sliding lower. She grasped the swelling heat pressing against the fabric of his pants, eliciting a deep groan that vibrated through her own body.

"Elena…" Logan's voice was ragged, a plea laced with need.

"Shh," she murmured, her lips trailing a path of soft kisses along the sharp line of his jaw. "Let go. Let me take care of you."

Her fingers worked quickly, undoing the clasp of his belt with practiced ease. The heavy fabric slid down his legs, revealing the thick, pulsing length that demanded her full attention. For a moment, she simply took him in—her breath catching at the raw, undeniable beauty of him.

Then, with deliberate and languid intent, she began to explore him, savoring each detail as though he were something rare and precious—an exquisite secret meant to be unraveled slowly and reverently. Her gaze lingered for a heartbeat, tracing every line, every curve, before she lowered her head with unhurried grace. Her lips parted softly, a breath of warmth preceding their tender closure around him, sealing him within a gentle heat that drew him deeper into her embrace.

The velvet slickness of her mouth enveloped him completely, cocooning him in sensation that was at once soothing and incendiary. Her tongue moved with patient artistry, slow, teasing swirls that both caressed and commanded, loosening the tightly coiled threads of his restraint strand by strand. Every flick, every delicate press was deliberate, a language unspoken but powerfully understood.

Logan's eyes fluttered shut, lashes trembling against his cheeks as a low, involuntary groan slipped from him—raw, unguarded, impossible to suppress. His chest rose and fell in uneven waves, the tension inside him dissolving under her measured rhythm, melting into a helpless surrender. Each motion of her hands, guiding and stroking with flawless harmony alongside her mouth, reinforced the intimacy of her hold over him. It was a rhythm of possession and devotion, steady and inexorable, drawing him further into the spell she wove around his body and spirit.

"Oh, Elena..." His voice was ragged, a whispered symphony of pleasure and release.

She reveled in the delicious control, the intoxicating intimacy of holding him so completely, as though every fiber of his body and will belonged solely to her in that moment. With deliberate precision, she quickened her pace— measured, purposeful, never hurried—her hand stroking in perfect harmony with the sensual rhythm of her mouth. The coordination was seamless, a dance of devotion and desire, each movement heightening the hunger that pulsed and deepened between them.

Logan's breath broke into ragged gasps, harsh and uneven, the sound of a man fraying at the edges of restraint. His body arched beneath her, muscles taut and trembling, the heat of his need radiating against her like a living flame. She could feel the tremors building in him, the sharp pull of tension that spoke of surrender just out of reach—until at last he let go, shattering with a guttural cry as he spilled hot and heavy into her.

Elena welcomed him without hesitation, savoring the rush with quiet triumph, her touch both gentle and unyielding as she guided him through the crest of release. She did not stop, her movements easing only when the last tremor drained from his body, when his ragged gasps softened into something slower, steadier.

Only then did she ease him down, her hands tender, her presence unwavering, lingering with him in the quiet aftershocks. The air around them seemed charged, still trembling with the sparks of closeness, each shimmer of connection binding them more tightly together than before.

Slowly, she rose, lips seeking his again in a kiss that shifted from fierce to tender—a soft connection brimming with unspoken promises. Their foreheads rested together, breaths mingling, hearts tentatively syncing.

Logan's usual stoicism fell away, his carefully constructed armor slipping until she glimpsed the rawness beneath. The sight of it—his vulnerability laid bare—made her chest ache with a tenderness so sharp it was almost pain. Without hesitation, he drew her into his arms, pulling her close with a force that felt less like possession and more like desperation, as if holding her tightly was the only way to anchor them both against the storm within him.

She lifted her hand to his face, her fingers tracing the rugged line of his jaw before coming to rest against his cheek. Her touch lingered there, gentle yet steady, a quiet tether holding him in place. The warmth of his skin beneath her palm was alive, fragile in its humanity, and she let herself savor the rare gift of this unguarded moment.

"You keep so much locked away," she whispered, her voice trembling with both sorrow and hope. Her gaze searched his, willing him to see the truth she had carried with her all along. "But what we have—it's been there from the start. Tell me you feel it too."

For a heartbeat, Logan said nothing. The silence between them felt taut, heavy with all the things he had never spoken. His jaw tightened as if fighting words, he didn't trust himself to release. Then, finally, his eyes softened—just enough.

"Elena..." His voice was low, rough with restraint. "I've tried not to. God knows I've tried. Because the moment I admit it, the moment I let it out—it changes everything. And I don't know if I can protect you the way I should if I let myself want you the way I do."

The confession hung in the air, dangerous and tender all at once. A thrill sparked within Elena's chest, courage blooming with quiet certainty.

A thrill sparked within Elena's chest, courage blooming with quiet certainty. "Then stop fighting," she urged, fingers threading through his hair. "I don't want you holding back— not from me."

Logan's hands tightened on her waist, the flicker of restraint fading like embers in a breeze. His voice was low, rough with emotion. "Are you sure, Elena?"

She smiled again, fierce and unwavering. "Surer than anything I've ever known."

Outside, the fire burned low, its warm glow cocooning them in a sanctuary of stolen time. The world beyond the cabin walls—the threats, the danger, the unknown—felt distant, muted by the steady rhythm of their shared breaths and the fragile peace settling between them.

In this moment, beneath the flush of firelight and whispered promises, Elena let herself believe they could face whatever came next. Together.

Chapter 6: A Fragile Plan

Morning arrived too quickly, sunlight slipping through the cabin's wooden blinds in honeyed streaks that spilled across the worn floorboards. Elena stirred beneath the gentle heat, reluctant to leave the warmth of Logan's steady arms. Her cheek pressed softly against his chest, the steady thump of his heartbeat a quiet anchor amidst the fragile calm.

For a moment, time paused—birdsong drifted lazily through the open window, leaves whispering in a gentle breeze. The world beyond felt muted, suspended in the soft glow of early light. But the illusion shattered as the weight of reality crept in like a shadow at the edge of dawn. Donovan was still out there, a looming specter threatening to unravel everything—every fragile alliance, every thread of trust painstakingly woven, every piece of damning evidence risking exposure.

Elena shifted, slowly peeling away the last tendrils of sleep, stretching the stiffness from her limbs with slow, deliberate movements. Her voice was low, barely above a whisper. "Morning."

"Morning," Logan answered, his tone rough around the edges but warm—steady like the promise it carried.

She offered a brief, tight smile before the heaviness of their mission settled back over her like a second skin. "We need to decide our next move," she said, voice steady but charged with urgency.

Logan's gaze sharpened, the weight of long nights and difficult choices settling behind his eyes. "Donovan's network is layered—shell companies hiding dirty money, offshore accounts beyond reach, corrupt officials turning blind eyes, arms dealers fueling his empire. Every piece is designed to keep him two steps ahead of the law. But even the most intricate webs have weak points. Our job is to find them and pull—hard."

Elena's jaw tensed as she absorbed his words, the fire of conviction flaring behind her eyes. "He has to be stopped. For good," she said, voice firm, nearly a vow.

The cabin had become their refuge—a fragile sanctuary carved out of the chaos, a quiet island amid the raging storm that battered against its walls. Inside, the fire crackled low, casting flickering shadows across the worn wood, but the warmth could not fully chase away the knowledge that beyond this thin shelter, the battle still waited, patient and unrelenting. Every heartbeat of silence felt borrowed, each breath stolen from the relentless tide pressing in on them.

Leaning forward, her elbows braced against the scarred wooden table, Elena's hands clasped tightly as if the act alone might steady her resolve. Her eyes, lit by the glow of the fire, burned with a fierce determination that cut through the heavy stillness. The sharp edge in her voice carried both urgency and finality as she broke the fragile quiet.

"No more waiting," she said, each word deliberate, striking like flint. "It's time to get to work."

Their eyes met—silent agreements passing between them like electricity—before they turned toward the scattered files and laptops strewn across the table. Together, they began unraveling the tangled threads of Donovan's empire, their shared purpose a quiet counterpoint to the chaos that threatened to consume them.

**

The late morning sun filtered softly through the cabin windows, casting warm golden beams across the cluttered table where Elena worked relentlessly. Her laptop screen was a maze of spreadsheets and encrypted files—each coded line and encrypted folder a fragile thread that could unravel the vast, shadowy empire Donovan had built. The faint scent of pine from the open window mingled with the sharp tang of cold coffee forgotten at her side.

Across the room, Logan paced near the kitchen counter, the tight set of his jaw betraying the quiet storm inside. His voice, low and urgent, sliced through the steady hum of the heater as he spoke into his phone. "I don't care about the cost. I want every detail on Donovan's overseas accounts and movements. He's tied to something bigger. Get me everything." After a tense pause, his tone dropped lower, threading grit with command. "Send the files through the secure line. And make it fast."

When he ended the call, his eyes locked onto Elena's—dark, hard, burdened. She could see the weight pressing down on him, the invisible ledger of risk and loss they carried. Her voice was steady but laced with an edge of unease. "What did they say?"

Logan exhaled slowly, jaw clenched as if trying to contain the dread flickering beneath his surface. "It's worse than we imagined." His gaze sharpened, speaking volumes without words. "Donovan's been funneling millions through a labyrinth of shell companies scattered across continents—a web crafted to disappear into shadows. But there's a crack… a break in the chain."

Elena leaned forward instinctively, pulse hiking with a mix of hope and alarm. "What kind of break?"

"A whistleblower," Logan said, not averting his eyes. "Someone inside flagged suspicious transactions linked to illicit arms deals. The tip came in from Europe just hours ago. If we can convince this person to come forward… it could shatter Donovan's entire operation."

Her throat tightened, breath quickening. "That's… huge. But it's dangerous. If Donovan finds out—"

"He won't," Logan cut in, firm as stone. "Not if we move fast and stay careful. But the clock is ticking."

The room slipped into tense silence, punctuated only by the steady hum of the heater and the faint rustling of pages stacked nearby. Elena's fingers curled around her coffee mug, the warmth a fragile tether to the moment as her mind raced—torn between the fragile flicker of hope this lead offered and the looming threat shadowing it. Quietly, she asked, "What if this is our only chance? What if this whistleblower is the key to stopping him—for good?

Logan stepped closer, his presence steady and unyielding. "Then we make it count. Every move must be precise. But I need you to trust me, Elena. This hunt… it won't be easy. And it won't be safe."

Her eyes searched his—finding not just determination but a shared vulnerability beneath his hardness. "I trust you," she said softly, voice nearly breaking with the weight of what lay ahead. "I hate feeling… powerless."

His expression softened, and slower than the rest, his hand reached up to brush a rough thumb along her cheek. The contact grounded her, a balm against the swirling doubt. "You're not powerless—not ever. You're fighting just as hard. And I promise you, we will take him down. Together."

Elena nodded, a flicker of fierce resolve sparking in her chest, chasing away some of the cold creeping in from outside. Whatever dangers waited beyond these walls; she would face them—with him at her side.

***

The soft, amber glow of dusk settled over the cabin, filtering through the windows and casting elongated shadows that danced lightly across the worn wooden dining table. Elena spread a scatter of papers before her—maps dog-eared and marked with hastily scrawled notes, data sheets peppered with highlights and margin jottings. The faint scent of pine and burning wood hung in the air, mingling with the crisp tang of late autumn as the evening deepened.

Across from her, Logan's laptop screen shimmered with a complex web of routes and figures. He leaned forward, finger tracing a highlighted line that snaked across the map. "If Donovan's offshore accounts tie to this corridor," he said, voice steady but edged with urgency, "we could have a direct lead. But we have to move fast—before he covers his tracks."

Elena's eyes stayed locked on the map for a long moment, the weight of every possibility settling into her bones. Then she shifted her gaze to Logan—his jaw set, eyes sharp, every movement deliberate. Amid the storm of uncertainty swirling around them, his unwavering focus anchored her. She hadn't anticipated leaning so heavily on anyone, least of all now, when the stakes felt unbearably high. Yet his quiet strength, the steady rhythm of his calm amidst the chaos, had become a lifeline she hadn't realized she needed.

Without thinking, her hand reached out, brushing lightly against his. The touch was simple, almost hesitant—but it spoke volumes. "Thank you. For everything."

Logan looked up, the tension that had etched his face softening in that shared moment. "You don't have to thank me," he said quietly, a slow, genuine smile tugging at the corners of his mouth. "We're in this together."

His words lingered, settling like a pulse between them in the dimming light. For Elena, it crystallized a truth she hadn't fully faced—his presence wasn't just a comfort, not merely a shield against danger. It was essential. An unspoken promise that no matter how dark the path ahead, she wouldn't walk it alone.

In the hush that followed, the fragile connection between them deepened, weaving taut threads of trust and resolve— a quiet vow to stand united against whatever came next.

Chapter 7: Into the Lion's Den

The sanctuary of the cabin slipped away, replaced by the cold, unyielding reality of their mission. For a fleeting moment, Elena and Logan had found something rare—a fragile comfort in each other—but Donovan's shadow stretched long and threatening, reminding them how high the stakes had become.

Logan's footsteps echoed softly against the worn hardwood floor as he paced the living room, the late morning sunlight filtering through faded curtains. The pale gold light warmed the space but did little to ease the suffocating weight pressing on them both—like a calm before a storm that refused to break. Elena sat rigid at the table, laptop open before her, her eyes scanning lines of encrypted files and financial data. Her fingers hovered, hesitant as if caught between hope and despair, her mind racing to keep pace with the mounting pressure.

Suddenly, Logan's phone buzzed sharply against the wooden surface, shattering the fragile silence. He answered immediately, voice quick and taut. "Chase here."

The reply was brisk, unmistakably official. "Agent Walters, FBI. We've got a situation. Can you and Congresswoman Delgado come to HQ? There's a break in the Donovan case—we need her testimony right away."

Elena's heartbeat quickened, her gaze snapping to Logan's face, searching for clues beneath his tightening jaw and narrowed eyes.

"What kind of break?" Logan demanded; voice low but sharp.

"One of Donovan's men flipped," Walters explained, urgency threading through every word. "We have corroborating evidence—but we need her signature on a warrant. It's critical."

Logan's shoulders stiffened; he ended the call with a terse, "We'll head out within the hour." His eyes met Elena's, a silent conversation passing between them—equal parts hope and unspoken caution.

"What's the situation?" she asked, words barely steady.

"There's a lead," Logan said, voice measured. "They want us back in D.C.— immediately."

Elena's chest tightened with a surge of tentative optimism. "This could be it," she breathed — "the break we've been chasing."

But beneath Logan's composed exterior, a flicker of seasoned wariness glimmered in his eyes. Years in the field had taught him how quickly hope could twist into danger. "Maybe," he said carefully, pacing with purpose, "or this could be a trap."

Her excitement faltered, confusion tightening her brow. "A trap? Why would they set that?"

He stopped, folding his arms against his chest as if bracing against an unseen blow. "Donovan's reach runs deep— through the system, through people we don't even know. If he senses we're closing in, he could use this 'break' to lure us out, to isolate us."

Elena's mind spun, weighing the risks and rewards in an instant. "But what if it isn't? What if this truly is our shot to stop him?"

Logan ran a hand through his thick hair, jaw clenched in frustration and concern. "That's what we have to figure out. We'll go. But we don't walk into this blindly. Not without eyes wide open."

***

The drive back to D.C. hummed with a strained silence tighter than the narrow stretch of road ahead. Elena's fingers absently twisted a slender silver bracelet over her wrist, the cold metal a small anchor amid the swirl of uneasy thoughts choking her. Outside, the world blurred past in muted shades—the trees, the fading sky—but her gaze was fixed somewhere beyond the glass, tangled in a thicket of fears.

Logan's occasional glances toward the rearview mirror punctuated the stillness, each one a reminder that no one's watching was safe. Finally, his voice cut through the quiet, low and cautious. "You're quiet."

Elena hesitated, swallowing down the tightening knot in her throat. "Just thinking," she admitted, voice barely above a murmur. "If this is a trap... what's the endgame? What does Donovan stand to gain by dragging us back into the lion's den?"

Logan's grip around the steering wheel constricted, knuckles paling. "Leverage," he said flatly. "Or worse—getting rid of a problem."

His words pressed into her like ice, carving deeper at the fragile calm she had been clinging to. Ahead, the jagged silhouette of the city skyline etched against the sky brought no comfort—only a sharp contrast to the shadowed uncertainty consuming her.

Suddenly, without warning, Logan veered off the highway, tires crunching over loose gravel onto a narrow side road swallowed by thick woods. The sudden movement jolted Elena, her body instinctively stiffening. "What are you doing?" she asked, voice taut.

Logan's hand reached for his phone, fingers flicking across the screen with practiced ease. "Calling Nora."

Elena's lips pressed into a thin line. She'd heard enough about Nora—the woman who operated like a ghost in the background, Logan's trusted confidante and master of logistics and security. Elena had never met her, but something about the ease with which Logan leaned on Nora left a bitter taste in her mouth.

Her arms crossed, a subtle shield as she fixed her eyes on Logan's face, searching for answers beneath the calm veneer.

"Nora," Logan said the moment the call connected, voice clipped but steady. "We need an exit plan."

"Trouble?" Nora's voice was smooth, calm—confident in a way that suggested she thrived in chaos. "I was already suspicious when I caught wind of that warrant request. You think it's bait?"

"Possibly," Logan confessed, the edge in his voice softening. "Can you have a contingency ready?"

"Already in motion. I'll be in position by the time you get there."

Logan nodded, more to himself than anyone else. "If I give the signal, Elena excuses herself and meets you in the restroom. You get her out quietly. I'll stay behind, make sure she's not followed."

"Understood," Nora affirmed without hesitation. "A car will be waiting."

"Thanks, Nora," Logan said.

"Anytime, Chase," came the reply, laced with a familiarity that made Elena's skin prickle.

As Logan ended the call, she let a slow breath escape, trying to steady the sudden rush of protective instinct and prickling suspicion. "She seems… efficient," Elena said, voice tight but controlled.

Logan shot her a smirk, the faintest flash of amusement in his eyes. "She's the best. If we're going to get out of this, it's because of her."

Elena said nothing, just clenched her fingers tighter in her lap—an unspoken vow solidifying beneath the veneer of calm. In that charged silence, the stakes shrank neither in scale nor in shadow.

***

They arrived in D.C. under a heavy cloud of uncertainty. As Logan guided the car into the cavernous underground parking garage of the federal building, Elena felt a storm roaring beneath her calm facade. Since that tense phone call with Nora, unease had settled deep in her gut—irrational or not, the way Nora's presence so easily folded into Logan's life was unsettling, like a shadow she couldn't outrun.

Logan parked with practiced precision, then turned to her, voice low and steady but edged with quiet urgency. "Remember the plan. If I say, 'This doesn't add up,' excuse yourself to the restroom. Nora will be waiting."

Elena nodded tightly, forcing her breath to slow. "Understood."

They stepped out into the sterile chill of the building's interior. Almost instantly, an agent approached Logan, their exchange swift and hushed as the weight of their task pressed down in the tight space. Elena moved ahead, her steps measured but brisk, nerves tingling like static as she approached the main entrance.

A figure emerged from the shadows—a silhouette clad in black, every inch radiating control. Nora.

The sharp glint of Nora's eyes locked onto Elena's with deliberate coolness. "Nice to finally meet you, Congresswoman."

Elena folded her arms, the tension coiling in her shoulders. "Likewise."

Nora's smirk flickered—a blade veiled in silk. "Jealousy doesn't suit you," she said, voice dropping to a near whisper.

Elena stiffened; every muscle drawn taut. "Excuse me?"

"You think I don't see it?" Nora leaned in, breath barely stirring the air. "Logan trusts me. You don't like it. But trust isn't about liking. It's about reliability. And right now, I'm the one keeping you both alive."

Elena clenched her jaw so tightly the taste of iron filled her mouth. She refused to take the bait.

Nora straightened, the smirk sharpening into something colder, more commanding. "Now, if we're done with the silent standoff, let's focus on getting you out of here in one piece."

Elena exhaled sharply, turning away just as Logan approached. His eyes flicked between the two women, oblivious to the unspoken battle that had just played out.

"Everything good?" he asked, voice even.

"Perfect," Nora responded smoothly, already striding toward a back entrance. Elena swallowed the lump in her throat and followed Logan inside.

Agent Walters awaited down the hall, his posture stiff beneath the harsh glare of fluorescent lights that bounced cold reflections off the stacked files on the conference room table. The air was thick with stress—a pressing urgency Elena could almost taste.

"Have a seat," Walters gestured without warmth.

Elena lowered herself carefully into the chair, every movement controlled as she watched him slide a thick document across the table.

"This is the warrant," he said, voice clipped. "We've gathered enough evidence to proceed—but your signature is necessary."

Logan reached out, seizing the document before Elena's fingers could graze it. Walters opened his mouth to protest, but Logan's sharp glare silenced him.

Furrowing his brows, Logan scanned the warrant, lips barely moving as he muttered under his breath, "This doesn't add up."

The phrase shot through Elena's mind like a flare. Instinct barely allowing a pause, she straightened in her chair and glanced quickly toward the hallway. "Excuse me," she said, voice steady but urgent, and rose.

Inside the dim restroom, Nora waited—her presence immediate and unyielding. Without a word, she grabbed Elena's wrist, her hold firm but efficient, pulling her swiftly through a labyrinth of shadowed corridors. Outside a side exit, they slipped into a sleek black car. Nora opened the door with a sharp push. "Get in."

Elena obeyed without hesitation, heart hammering fiercely against her ribs. "What's happening?"

Nora ignored the question, settling behind the wheel and starting the engine with practiced calm. "Logan will fill you in when he meets us."

The car weaved through back roads, doubling back and twisting in a deliberate effort to shake any potential followers. Darkness cloaked them, the faint ticking of the cooling metal and Elena's own ragged breaths the only sounds breaking the tense silence.

They pulled into the underground garage of a nondescript office building. Time stretched, each minute a weight pressing deeper into Elena's throat, nerves fraying as she counted the seconds.

Finally, Logan's vehicle slid into the lot, merging smoothly beside Nora's car. "Go," Nora said, voice clipped.

Without hesitation, Elena slipped from one car to the other, settling into the passenger seat. She stole a glance at Logan's profile—the tight jaw, the furrowed brow—searching for answers that didn't come.

Logan sat silent, the tension hollow between them until Nora pulled away, winding their path in the opposite direction before he finally turned the key in the ignition.

Elena broke the quiet, voice sharp with frustration. "Logan, what was wrong with the warrant?"

His jaw clenched tighter. "Not now."

The finality in his tone extinguished her protest, but the fire within wouldn't be so easily doused.

"Logan—"

"We're heading back to the safe house," he cut her off, his voice leaving no room for argument. "We wait. No more risks until we know what we're dealing with."

Elena swallowed hard, the city lights blurring into streaks beyond the window—each one a reminder that whatever Logan saw had been enough to send them running. That knowledge terrified her far more than the danger itself.

"Logan—"

For a moment, the silence pressed heavy, the hum of the engine filling the void. Then Logan exhaled, a sound edged with restraint.

"They wanted you to sign that warrant," he said finally, his voice low, deliberate. "Not because it was necessary—but because it would tie *you* to it. Your signature would have made it look like you were complicit, like you were admitting to knowledge of everything inside that file. Walters wasn't just handing you a document—he was handing you a noose."

Her pulse spiked, heat rushing to her face. "You mean—if I'd signed—"

"It would've been the same as confessing to a crime you didn't commit," Logan said grimly, his eyes fixed on the road. "From that moment on, every headline, every investigation would've had your name inked beside Donovan's. And the people behind him would've had exactly what they wanted: you, silenced, dragged down with the rest."

Elena's throat tightened. Betrayal and relief tangled inside her chest, a bitter knot she could hardly swallow past. "So this was never about justice," she whispered.

Logan's jaw flexed. "It was about eliminating you."

Chapter 8: A Race Across the Sea

The pale glow of dawn seeped through the heavy curtains, smudging the boundaries between night and day. Elena sat on the faded sofa, fingers curled tightly around a chipped porcelain cup. The tea inside had long since cooled, forgotten, but its faint scent lingered—a fragile echo of normalcy she wasn't sure she deserved anymore.

Across the room, Logan's restless footsteps stirred the silence. He paced the length of the small space, his stride sharp and uneven, as though even the floor beneath them couldn't be trusted. His phone was pressed tightly to his ear, his voice clipped, low, taut with urgency.

"Yes," he said, his tone precise, leaving no room for hesitation. "We're ready. But the warrant's compromised— no delays, no questions, no paper trail." His jaw flexed, the line of stubble catching in the dim light as he ground the words out. A beat of silence followed, then: "Good. Make it happen."

The click of the call ending echoed too loudly in the still air.

When his eyes met hers, they were hard and unyielding, but beneath the stone mask, Elena caught the flicker of strain.

"We have the green light," he said quietly, as though speaking the words aloud might summon the danger lurking just beyond their walls. "Tonight."

Her breath caught, heart skipping. Dawn painted his features in pale light, illuminating the deep furrow etched between his brows.

"We don't have time to debate," he added, his voice tightening. "They've weaponized the law against you. That warrant—the one Walters shoved at us—it wasn't just flawed. It was doctored. Twisted to implicate you. If you'd signed it, Elena, it would've been the same as confessing. If we don't move fast, they'll have you in cuffs before anyone can blink."

The words sank into her like cold iron. "But Donovan—this can't be right," she whispered.

Logan raked a hand through his hair, tension shaking through him. "Right or not doesn't matter anymore. The law's the weapon now. And if you stay, you lose control."

Elena forced her hands to unclench, setting the porcelain cup onto the table. The soft clink sounded like a gavel in the silence. Normalcy was gone. Every comfort was an illusion now.

"How bad is this?" she asked, her voice steadier than she felt.

Logan crouched in front of her, closing the distance, his hands firm as they settled on her knees. The weight of them grounded her, anchoring her against the storm threatening to sweep her away. His scent—leather, charcoal, steel—wrapped around her, and for a moment, she clung to it like a lifeline.

She searched his face, desperate for certainty, but all she found was the thin tightrope between fear and resolve.

Her throat tightened. She swallowed hard and drew a slow, deliberate breath. "Then we leave," she said, her voice firm despite the tremor inside. "Tonight. Whatever it takes."

Logan's jaw flexed once more in reluctant agreement. His hands lingered a heartbeat longer before he stood, his posture stiffening back into the soldier she had first met.

"Wheels up in two hours," he said, his voice all steel now. He turned toward the window, narrowing his eyes as headlights cut across the drive. "Transport's here."

Two unmarked SUVs rolled to a stop outside, engines low, deliberate. A small detail of federal agents climbed out, moving with sharp precision. Logan didn't relax until he recognized the faces—men and women he trusted, pulled from outside the usual channels to avoid the taint of Donovan's influence.

He turned back to Elena. "They'll take us to the airfield. No mistakes. Keep your head down."

A knock rattled the safe house door, brisk and professional. Logan's hand hovered instinctively near his weapon as he cracked it open, scanning the faces before swinging it wider to admit the lead agent.

The team slipped inside with efficient silence, the room's air shifting with their presence. Elena rose, pulse hammering, the fragile calm she'd clung to shattering under the weight of reality. Every step they took now pressed her closer to the line she could never uncross.

***

Engines rumbled low outside as the agents guided them into the waiting SUVs. Elena slid into the backseat beside Logan, the leather cold against her palms. One agent took the driver's seat, another the front passenger, their movements efficient, watchful.

The convoy rolled out, headlights slicing through the morning mist. The silence in the vehicle was thick—broken only by the hum of tires on pavement and the clipped exchanges over radios. Every turn, every crawl at an intersection, made Elena's pulse climb higher. She pressed her forehead lightly to the glass, scanning the empty roads as if shadows themselves might lunge from the tree line.

Logan sat rigid at her side, his hand resting near his weapon. His gaze flicked constantly—side mirrors, rooftops, dark alleys sliding past. He was cataloging every angle of attack, every threat she couldn't see.

The agents in front spoke only in fragments:

"Clear."

"Two cars back, dark sedan—hold position."

"Adjusting route."

Elena's heart skipped. "What sedan?" she whispered, fingers tightening on the folder in her lap.

Logan's reply was low, meant only for her. "Probably nothing. But we don't assume." His eyes stayed locked on the mirrors.

The convoy made a sharp turn, tires crunching over gravel as they diverted down a narrower road. The sedan followed—too close, headlights flaring in the rear window. Elena's breath caught.

"Confirmation?" the driver muttered into his mic.

"Stand by," came the reply from the SUV behind them. Seconds stretched like hours. Then: "Sedan's turning off. False alarm. Clear."

Relief rippled through the vehicle, but Logan didn't relax. His hand lingered near his weapon, jaw locked tight.

Elena forced a breath past the knot in her throat. "You think it was coincidence?"

His eyes stayed on the road ahead, voice flat. "I don't believe in coincidence."

The convoy pressed on, engines humming low. Gravel crunched beneath the tires as the treeline opened to reveal the faint silhouette of a hangar. The SUV slowed, headlights spilling over a sleek private jet waiting on the cracked tarmac, engines already alive with a steady hum.

The sight of it struck her with a sudden, surreal weight. This wasn't just leaving Washington. This was stepping into the unknown.

Logan leaned close, his voice pitched only for her. "When those doors open, we move fast. Straight to the jet. No hesitation."

She swallowed hard and nodded, pulse thundering in her ears.

The agent in the front seat turned. "Perimeter's clear. Let's go."

The doors opened. Cold air rushed in, sharp with jet fuel and dawn's chill. Logan's hand pressed firmly against her back, steady, guiding.

For one breathless instant, as the jet loomed before her, Elena thought: This is the point of no return.

***

The private jet thrummed quietly as it sliced through the night sky, the city's scattered lights shrinking into distant, flickering sparks beneath a blanket of darkness. Elena pressed her forehead lightly against the cool glass, staring out at the void that seemed to mirror the weight settling in her chest. Resting on her lap was the thin folder holding the whistleblower's files—a fragile thread tethering her to hope and danger both. The faint rustle of papers inside was the only sound breaking the low hum of the engines.

Across the aisle, Logan sat motionless, his jaw clenched as his thumb scrolled through urgent messages on his phone. The pale glow from the screen cast sharp angles over his face, revealing shadows deeper than the faint lines of fatigue.

Though his expression remained controlled, something raw simmered just beneath—an urgency Elena felt more than saw.

After a pause, Logan's voice cut through the quiet, softer than before. "You holding up?"

She blinked, then turned toward him, forcing a small, tight smile. "Funny to think that seven days ago, I was pushing for policy reform briefs. Now, I'm halfway across the world chasing down criminals."

His lips curved, a ghost of humor flickering in the tired lines. "That's a detour you never added to your résumé, huh?"

A breathy laugh escaped her, unexpected and fragile. "Not even close." She shifted, the hum of the jet vibrating through her fingers. "But… I'm relieved it's not just me in this."

Their eyes locked, the space between them shrinking as the noise of the outside world dimmed to a whisper. Logan reached out, fingers curling gently over hers—a grounding anchor in the storm swirling around them.

"We'll get through it," he said, voice low but steady.

Elena swallowed hard, the lump in her throat tightening as conflicting emotions churned—was it fear? Hope? She couldn't tell. But in that fleeting moment of shared quiet, she let herself cling to that promise, fragile as the dawn waiting just beyond the horizon.

***

The jet's wheels ground against the cracked tarmac of a remote airstrip just as dawn stretched its first tentative fingers across the sky, painting the horizon in fragile shades of pink and orange. A sharp, biting chill sliced through Elena's layered clothes the moment she stepped outside, the cold biting at her skin beneath the fabric. Mist curled low over the grass, swirling in ghostly wisps around two black SUVs parked a short distance away, their dark forms stark against the pale light.

Drivers stood beside the vehicles, scanning the surroundings with restless, hawk-like eyes, muscles taut beneath their leather jackets. One of them stepped forward as Logan opened her door, voice low and steady. "Safe house is about an hour from here. The perimeter's tight, but nothing's foolproof. Stay sharp."

Elena slid into the backseat, the stiff leather biting at her wrists. As Logan closed the door behind her, his hand brushed briefly against her back—a silent current of reassurance that ignited a fleeting spark of warmth amid the morning's chill.

"Stay alert," his voice murmured close, heavy with unspoken warning.

The convoy shifted onto narrow country roads, the dense trees lining the path like silent sentinels. Dawn's soft light filtered through branches, dappling the road with fleeting patches of gold and shadow. Elena's gaze flicked involuntarily between the passing trunks and the darker thickets beyond—each bend threatening to conceal unseen eyes. The crisp morning air was thick with tension, each breath sharp but hollow.

Her voice was barely above a whisper when she finally spoke, "What's the plan once we get there?"

Logan's jaw clenched as he kept his eyes fixed on the road, "We secure the whistleblower first. Then we comb through the evidence, make sure it holds. After that, we don't linger. Donovan can't know we're moving."

She tightened her grip on the worn folder resting in her lap, nails digging into the edges. "This has to work, Logan. If it doesn't, everything falls apart."

His steady reply didn't quite reach his eyes. "It will." But the flicker of doubt lurking behind his gaze mirrored the gnawing unease twisting low in her gut.

***

The safe house stood sentinel at the edge of a grove, its weathered stone facade half-hidden behind trees aflame with autumn's fire—leaves blistering in shades of red and orange, crackling softly in the crisp morning air. The vibrant colors seemed almost too vivid against the muted strength of the house, an ancient bastion holding secrets as old as the land itself.

Inside, pale light filtered through tall windows, casting long, restless shadows. The whistleblower, a gaunt man in threadbare clothes, paced nervously by the window, his thin frame a fragile silhouette against the pale glow. His hands trembled, both from fatigue and fear, as they brushed over a scattered stack of documents and a worn flash drive resting on the scarred wooden table.

"Thank you for coming," he said, voice tight with tension. "I've got the whole network laid out—the money transfers, offshore accounts, the names you need. But Donovan's men… they're watching everywhere. We're not just unsafe; we're hunted."

Elena stepped forward, forcing strength into her voice when all she felt was the raw ache of exhaustion. "We're here to protect you. There won't be time to turn back. The truth has to come out."

The whistleblower's gaze flicked to Logan, suspicion etching his weary face. His eyes searched Logan's with blatant mistrust, unspoken worries. Logan met that gaze without flinching, his tone measured and steady. "You're safe here. We've planned every angle, but this depends on you—staying strong, staying alive."

A long beat — then the whistleblower's shoulders eased slightly, the tension melting into reluctant acceptance.

Elena felt the oppressive weight of the moment settle like a stone in her gut. There was no room for doubt. Not now. Not ever.

They bent over the documents together, peeling back layers of Donovan's corruption like peeling back skin to reveal the rot beneath. Offshore accounts funneling untold sums, officials bought and silenced, illegal deals etched across ledger pages. With every page Elena turned, her hands trembled harder—this wasn't just evidence. It was a ticking fuse.

"This is it," Logan said low, leaning close enough that his breath brushed warm against her ear, a fragile comfort against the cold dread.

Elena nodded, heartbeat pounding a frantic rhythm. "Now we just have to survive long enough to expose it."

Logan's hand settled firmly on her shoulder; a silent vow wrapped in his steady grip. "We've got this," he said, voice rough but certain. "No matter the cost."

Before she could answer, a sharp knock rattled the door. An agent stepped inside, face grim, voice clipped. "Sir—chatter confirms movement. Donovan's men may have tracked the signal. We need to move. Now."

Logan's jaw tightened, the calm in his eyes turning to flint. He snapped the folder shut, tucking it securely under his arm as he rose. "Prep the convoy. Wheels up in thirty minutes."

The whistleblower's thin frame stiffened, his voice cracking with fear. "Tracked? If they know I talked—if they know I gave you this—I'm dead. Do you hear me? Dead!"

"Not tonight," Logan said flatly, his voice cutting like a blade.

The whistleblower's breathing quickened, his hands shaking as he tried to gather the scattered papers. Elena moved closer, her tone softer, steadying. "Listen to me. You've come this far because you want the truth to matter. You're not alone anymore. We're getting you out."

His frantic eyes searched hers, clinging to the anchor in her calm, before he gave a reluctant nod.

Within moments, the safe house was in motion—agents clearing rooms, securing exits, voices carrying sharp orders. Logan herded Elena and the whistleblower toward the rear door, his hand steady against Elena's back, his gaze never still. Engines rumbled outside, headlights cutting through the mist.

***

The three of them slid into the waiting SUV—Elena pressed between Logan and the whistleblower. His leg bounced incessantly, his hands twisting together until his knuckles whitened. Every few seconds he muttered under his breath: "They'll come. They'll find us."

"Breathe," Elena urged, gripping his arm just firmly enough to still him. "You're safe here."

"You don't know them," he hissed. "Donovan's reach—he has men everywhere."

Logan's eyes cut over, cold steel in the dim light. "Then let them try. They won't get within a mile."

The whistleblower swallowed, falling into uneasy silence, though the tremor in his shoulders didn't fade.

The convoy pressed on, headlights slashing through mist. Radios crackled with terse updates:

"Clear."

"Two dark sedans—hold their position."

"Adjust the route."

Elena's heart jolted. The whistleblower twisted toward her, panic sparking again. "It's them—I told you, they're here—"

"Quiet," Logan snapped. "We don't assume." His hand shifted to his weapon; eyes locked on the mirrors.

The convoy veered down a narrow service road. For three long turns, the sedan followed—until finally it peeled off onto another route. The trailing SUV confirmed, "False alarm. Clear."

Relief rippled through the vehicle, but Logan's jaw stayed tight. "I don't believe in coincidence," he muttered.

The whistleblower slumped against the seat, muttering, "We're already dead," before Elena caught his arm again, grounding him with a look that carried more steel than she felt. "No. Not dead. Not tonight."

***

The tree line broke to reveal the hangar, the private jet waiting with engines already alive, lights casting long beams across cracked tarmac.

The SUVs screeched to a halt. Doors opened. Cold air rushed in, cutting sharp and merciless. Agents spilled out, fanning in formation. Two moved ahead, scanning shadows, rifles low but ready.

The whistleblower hesitated at the SUV door, frozen in place. "I can't—I can't—"

Elena grabbed his hand firmly, pulling him out into the cold. "Yes, you can. One step at a time. We're almost there."

Logan pressed close on his other side, voice low and lethal. "Move. If you stop, you die here."

That snapped him forward, stumbling into motion.

Boots crunched on tarmac, mist curling low. A sharp metallic crack rang out from the hangar wall, weapons raised in an instant. Just a chain clattering loose in the wind. Still— the whistleblower nearly bolted until Elena's grip steadied him.

"At the stairs," the lead agent called. "All clear. Go."

Logan guided them quickly, his hand steady at Elena's back. At the base of the stairway, the whistleblower froze again, eyes darting wildly to the shadows.

Elena leaned close; her voice fierce but quiet. "This is your chance to make everything you've risked mean something. Go."

He swallowed hard, then climbed.

At the top, Elena ducked into the cabin, the hum of the jet swallowing her. Logan followed with the whistleblower; the cabin door sealing shut with a metallic thud.

For the first time in hours, Elena exhaled—but the weight in her chest never left.

Chapter 9: Shadows of Doubt

The plane droned steadily through the thick night, its engines a constant heartbeat beneath the heavy silence that clung to Elena. She pressed her forehead lightly against the cool window, eyes tracing the shadowed expanse of the ocean far below. Its dark surface seemed to swallow every flicker of light—a mirror to the turmoil swirling in her mind. In the distance, a faint shimmer marked the coastline, a fragile promise of landfall but no promise of safety. With every mile, the weight of what lay ahead settled deeper in her chest—a looming confrontation she both dreaded and was compelled to face.

Across the aisle, Logan sat with practiced ease, fingers moving methodically over his phone's screen. Yet his eyes never truly relaxed; the flicker of alertness was a silent testament to the storm brewing beneath his calm exterior. Elena wondered if he carried the same burden—the suffocating pressure of a mission that seemed impossible to outrun, like the gray clouds pressing against the plane's windows.

In the row behind, the whistleblower sat hunched forward, elbows braced on his knees, his hands twisting together. His restless movements created a jittery rhythm, a nervous percussion that grated against the drone of the engines. He muttered to himself in broken fragments, eyes darting to every sound as though the plane itself might betray them.

Elena turned slightly; her voice low but steady. "You're safe here. We're in the air. Donovan can't reach you."

The man shook his head, hollow eyes wild with doubt. "You don't understand. He has people everywhere. Pilots. Agents. Judges. If he knows I talked—"

Logan's voice cut in, sharp and firm. "He doesn't know. And he won't. This jet isn't on any manifest. No one is tracking us but my people. You'll live to see him fall—if you keep it together."

The whistleblower's mouth closed with a snap, but his leg still bounced in unspent panic.

Elena pressed her hand over the folder in her lap. She could feel his fear seeping into her own bones, a reminder of how fragile their position really was. Suspended in the air, between ground and destination, they were a moving target she prayed Donovan hadn't already marked.

"You've been quiet," Logan said after a while, his voice softening when it returned to her.

She offered a faint, frayed smile. "Just… thinking. About what's waiting for us. About how much everything's changed."

He set his phone down, giving her his full attention. "Changed how?"

Her voice faltered. "A week ago, my biggest concern was pushing policy reform. Now, I'm carrying proof that could take down a criminal empire. It doesn't feel real."

Logan's lips curved into a small, knowing smile. "You never signed up for this. But you're handling it better than most would."

Her eyes dropped to her lap, fingers twisting in her skirt. "But what if it's not enough? What if I'm not enough?"

Leaning forward, Logan locked eyes with her, conviction hard and unshakable. "You are. Donovan knows it, too. That's why he's so desperate to destroy you."

His words lit a fragile ember inside her, a spark of belief she hadn't dared hold in days. For the first time, she let herself think she might face what was coming and win.

The plane jolted softly as its wheels struck the tarmac, pulling her back into the present. Cold night air rushed in as the door opened, biting after the warmth of the cabin.

Agents moved first, ushering the whistleblower down the stairs. He hesitated, glancing back at Elena, his voice barely a whisper: "Don't let them bury the truth."

Her throat tightened, but she managed a steady nod. "I won't."

He disappeared into a waiting SUV, flanked by agents who melted into the darkness with him. One agent turned back to

Logan with a curt nod. "We'll handle him. Secured location. No tails."

Logan returned the nod. Then he placed a hand at the small of Elena's back, guiding her toward the terminal with protective precision.

Inside, the near-empty space hummed with fluorescent stillness. As they passed a shuttered coffee stand, a flickering television above it burst into sound:

"In breaking news, Congresswoman Elena Delgado, once a rising star in Washington, is now at the center of a corruption scandal."

Elena froze. On the screen, her own face glared back, framed by bold headlines screaming betrayal: **Congresswoman Delgado Accused of Corruption.**

Her heart slammed, blood draining from her face as the anchor rattled off accusations—offshore accounts, shell companies, fraudulent transfers. Grainy images of incriminating documents flashed in brutal succession, each one a blade cutting deeper.

"This can't be real," Elena whispered, her voice breaking. "It has to be Donovan. This is his play."

Logan shifted closer, angling his body to block her from curious stares. His jaw clenched, muscles tight beneath the stubble. His voice was low, urgent but controlled. "We don't stop. We move. Now."

Moments later, she and Logan were loaded into another SUV. The agents drove in silence, their eyes sharp, scanning every car and shadow as the convoy threaded into the city. Elena's grip on the folder whitened her knuckles, every page inside a reminder of what Donovan stood to lose—and what she stood to gain if she survived.

"He's trying to bury me," she muttered, voice thick with fury beneath her fear. "Turn me into the villain."

Logan's hand tightened—not on the wheel, but on the seat edge, body taut with vigilance as he scanned the passing streets. "Then we bury him deeper. But first, I get you safe."

By the window, Elena's reflection shimmered against the blur of city lights—fractured, layered, almost unrecognizable. A coil of anger twisted beneath her fear, forging resolve. She would not let Donovan win.

The SUV slowed, crunching over gravel, stopping outside a safe house hidden at the edge of a grove ablaze with autumn's fire—trees bleeding red and gold, their brittle leaves whispering warnings in the night air.

Logan exited first, scanning the perimeter, hand brushing the holster at his side. Agents flanked them quickly, securing the grounds with silent precision.

Inside, Elena sank into a worn chair, exhaustion crashing through her body in waves. Logan stayed close, his presence steady, grounding.

"You're stronger than you think," he told her, voice quiet but sure.

She met his gaze, voice raw. "I don't feel strong. Not right now."

His expression softened, though his eyes never wavered. "Strength isn't about how you feel. It's about what you do anyway."

Her hand brushed over the folder resting on the table—their weapon, the key to dismantling Donovan's empire. "This evidence... it's more than proof. It's my defense. It's the only way to show I'm not the monster he's painting me as."

Logan nodded once, firm and resolute. "Then we stay ahead of him. Donovan won't stop, so neither do we."

A knock shattered the moment. An agent stepped in, grim-faced. "There's chatter. His men might have tracked us here. Prep to move immediately."

Logan's jaw set, eyes narrowing. "Understood."

When the agent left, Logan turned back to her. "Are you ready?"

Elena rose, fear burning into steel. "Let's finish this."

The convoy rolled into the night. Elena sat rigid, the folder heavy in her lap. Beside her, Logan's body was taut, silent— her shield in the storm.

"Whatever happens," he said quietly, "I've got your back."

And in the darkness, with danger closing in, his words felt like armor.

Chapter 10: Safe House Passion

As the city lights dwindled behind them, Elena's eyes traced the shifting landscape outside—rolling Virginia hills bathed in the soft silver of a full moon. The moonlight spilled across fields like spilled milk, casting an ethereal glow over the tranquil countryside. It was a fragile peace, a stark contrast to the turmoil that had consumed her every waking thought.

She sat in the back seat of the SUV, gaze fixed on the dark ribbons of shadow chasing each other past the window, feeling the steady unraveling of the fierce resolve that had once carried her through every challenge. The calm outside only deepened the storm raging inside.

Every fragment of her mind circled back to Donovan's strike—her reputation shattered, her career crumbling like old stone. Everything she had built now seemed fragile, threadbare, beyond repair.

Across from her, Logan sat taut and watchful. The faint glow from the dashboard traced hard lines across his face, his eyes scanning the road through the windshield. He wasn't driving—an agent handled the wheel—but Logan's vigilance was as sharp as if the responsibility were his. Every mirror, every shift of the convoy's formation, his gaze cataloged it all.

"Elena," Logan's voice broke through the silence, low and steady, a tether pulling her back from the edge. "You're not alone in this. We'll get through it."

She turned toward him, her voice barely more than a breath. "It feels like it's over. Donovan's destroyed me—my reputation, my career. How can I even fight back?"

Logan leaned slightly forward; forearms braced on his knees. "This isn't just about you," he said, his tone threaded with iron. "It's about everyone Donovan's dragged down. All the people counting on us to stop him. He hasn't won. Not yet."

Her heart clenched. "But what if I'm not strong enough?"

For a fleeting moment, the armor he wore cracked, revealing something raw beneath. His voice softened, almost a whisper carrying unshakable conviction. "You are. And if you stumble, I'll be there to catch you. You're not in this alone."

His faith sparked a fragile ember inside her—hope flickering against the darkness.

The SUV slowed, crunching onto a gravel driveway that curved into shadow. Beyond the trees, a secluded safe house came into view, its weathered walls framed by crimson and gold leaves, windows spilling warm light across the night.

Engines idled as the convoy drew to a stop. Agents disembarked first, sweeping the grounds with silent precision before one of them opened Elena's door. Logan stepped out after her, his stance sharp, scanning the tree line with the ease of a man who had lived too long in danger.

When the lead agent gave the signal — "All clear"— he added, "We'll hold the perimeter until dawn, then rotate out. You're covered."

Logan gave a curt nod. "Understood."

Elena followed him up the path, the crunch of gravel loud beneath her heels. At the door, Logan opened it and extended his hand. For a moment, she hesitated—then took it. The brief contact steadied her against the swirling uncertainty, grounding her as the agents faded back into the night.

Inside, the door closed with a final thud, leaving them alone with the silence, the shadows, and the fragile promise of shelter.

***

Inside the safe house, the place's rustic charm felt almost cruelly out of place against the heaviness pressing down on them. The door clicked softly closed behind them, and as silence wrapped around Elena like a suffocating shroud, her carefully constructed facade cracked. She slid down the door, wrapping her arms tightly around her torso as if trying to hold herself together. Her breath hitched, chest tightening with a weight too heavy to carry alone. Her eyes shimmered with unshed tears, and a shaky exhale escaped her lips.

"I'm terrified, Logan," she whispered, voice fragile and breaking under the strain. "What if we can't stop him? What if everything we've fought for—everything I've fought for—is gone?"

Logan crossed the room in steady, purposeful strides, hands settling on her shoulders with a gentleness that belied their firmness. "We won't let that happen," he said, his voice unwavering, a quiet anchor in the storm. "Not now. Not after how far you've come."

That steadiness was the crack through which all her defenses collapsed. The tears she'd long held at bay spilled free, hot and unrelenting. She buried her face into his chest, trembling against him, the raw tension of months pouring out in convulsive sobs. Logan didn't speak—he simply held her, strong and still, absorbing the weight of her pain.

When the tremors finally eased, Elena pulled back enough to meet his gaze, eyes red-rimmed but sparkling with quiet gratitude. Her voice was raw. "Thank you… for being here. For knowing I'm not on my own."

Logan's thumb brushed a stray tear from her cheek, his own expression soft but fierce—reflecting the fierce tenderness that simmered beneath his calm exterior. "Always," he murmured, voice thick with something deeper than words. "You never will be."

They stood frozen in the stillness, the distance between them shrinking until it vanished, as an almost electric tension crackled in the charged space. Elena's heart drummed wild and loud beneath her ribs. For the first time in what felt like forever, she allowed herself to acknowledge the pull— undeniable and urgent—that had been quietly building between them. The moments they'd stolen, brief and charged, ignited a slow-burning fire that now blazed to life.

Without thinking, drawn by impulse and desire long buried beneath the weight of fear and duty, she leaned in. Her lips brushed his softly at first—a tentative question. Then, when his lips met hers fully, something inside her shifted and broke free. Flames stirred deep in her, fierce and alive.

Elena rose onto her toes, urgency sweeping through her like a current. She pressed forward, lips finding his again—this time with more intention. Her hands threaded into his hair, pulling him closer, her body melting against his with a heat that hummed between them. For a suspended moment, the scandal, the danger, the mission—all of it faded into a distant echo. There was only him, and the fire sparking wildly between them, burning away every fear and doubt.

Logan froze briefly, caught off guard, but then surrendered to the passion simmering beneath the surface for weeks. His hands cupped her face, thumbs gently brushing her cheeks, returning the kiss with a depth that matched her own hunger. Their lips moved together, exploration turning to possession—slow and demanding.

Elena's fingers tangled in the thick strands of his hair, tugging softly, tilting her head to deepen the kiss. Logan's hands slid lower, tracing the curve of her back, pulling her nearer, their bodies molding together perfectly—as if shaped by the same hands.

The kiss was a release—a surrender to the desire that had built quietly through stolen glances and suppressed moments. When they finally parted, breath held too long, Logan's hands roamed, mapping the contours of her waist and hips, drawing her tight against him. Elena's palms swept across his broad chest, the steady beat of his heart thrilling beneath her touch.

With a carefully measured nudge, Logan guided her toward the nearby couch. There, their kisses grew more urgent—less tentative, more commanding. He lowered her onto the soft cushions, his body arching over hers, eyes locked in a silent conversation of need and longing.

Elena's fingers deftly worked at the buttons of his shirt, exposing the firm planes beneath. Logan's breath hitched as her hands caressed bare skin, warm and electric. He mirrored her movements—fingers slipping beneath the straps of her dress, easing it down over her shoulders, revealing delicate lace against soft skin.

Disrobing became a frantic dance—clothes discarded hastily until only skin remained, bathed in the gentle glow of the lamp's amber light. Logan's eyes drank her in—the soft curves, the flushed skin, the rise and fall of her breath—before trailing kisses down her neck, coaxing soft sounds from her lips.

Elena's hands traced the powerful muscles of his back, nails pressing lightly, urging him closer. His lips found her breast, teasing through lace before daring to draw the fabric aside and claim her fully. Her back arched, hands clutching his hair, anchoring him as waves of pleasure rolled over her.

His mouth moved skillfully to her other breast, lavishing attention while one hand slid provocatively lower, fingers gliding along the sensitive skin of her inner thigh. Elena's breath grew ragged, body responding instinctively, hips rising to meet his touch.

"Logan…" she whispered; voice thick with desire.

Please…"

He didn't need the invitation. His fingers found her warmth, slipping easily inside, drawing gasps with every measured stroke. His thumb circled her most sensitive spot, building a rhythm that sent tremors through her core.

Elena's hands gripped the cushions harder, nails sinking into the fabric as she surrendered to the growing waves. Her hips moved in tandem with his hand, each motion a release of the tension that had bound her tight.

"Let go Elena," Logan murmured, breath hot against her ear. "Let go…"

His words shattered the last walls of restraint. Her body tensed, muscles coiling and releasing in an endless surge of pleasure. Her cry echoed through the room—a raw, shattering sound—as she tumbled over the edge, trembling and drenched in warmth.

Logan's touch softened, fingers tracing lazy circles as she slowly descended from the peak, his lips finding hers in a kiss sweet and gentle. "I've got you," he whispered, voice hoarse, thick with his own need. "Always."

Their arms tightened around one another; a silent promise sealed in the quiet heat of the safe house. Tomorrow, the fight would resume, but for now, they found solace, strength, and fierce connection in each other's embrace.

Chapter 11: Defiance in the Shadows

The first fragile light of dawn filtered through the blinds, casting long, restless shadows that stretched across the room like silent witnesses. Elena stirred beneath the tangled sheets, the night's weight still pressing down on her chest. The softness of sleep clung faintly, fragile as mist, until the sharp buzz of Logan's phone shattered the stillness. She watched him snatch it up, the easy calm draining from his face as his eyes darkened reading the screen.

"What's going on?" Elena's voice was hesitant, still touched by sleep as she pushed herself up, brushing unruly strands of hair from her face. But beneath the lingering drowsiness, a sharpened edge of anxiety crept in, quick and insistent.

"Nora," Logan muttered, swinging his legs off the bed with a fluid, almost mechanical grace. "Donovan's men are moving tonight—a warehouse in Baltimore. They're destroying evidence."

Her heart stuttered, the stark weight of his words settling over her like ice. Instinct surged, breath quickening. "Then we stop them."

Logan hesitated briefly, eyes clouded with a conflict she couldn't quite read. "Elena, this isn't a political maneuver or a press release. This is dangerous. People could die tonight."

A flicker of steel ignited inside her, smothering the thin embers of fear pushing at the edges. "That evidence is crucial, Logan. You need me. I'm going."

He spun to face her, jaw clenched tight, brows furrowed as if battling to hold his own storm in check. "No. You're not." His voice cracked sharp through the quiet, colder than she expected. "You stay where it's safe."

Something inside Elena snapped—a rush of indignation swelling in her chest. She pushed herself upright, bare feet meeting the cool floor with sure resolve, each step toward him a silent declaration. "You don't get to decide that for me. This is my fight, too."

"This isn't up for discussion!" Logan's words snapped back, edged with frustration and fear. The space between them crackled—charged with something raw and electric Elena struggled to name. His unspoken terror hovered, heavy and suffocating.

"I need to be there to identify the evidence," she insisted, voice firm despite the racing storm within.

Logan exhaled slowly, jaw tight like steel trapped beneath skin. "Fine. You can come. But you're wearing a vest. You stay in the van. You wait until we're done. No arguments. End of discussion."

The air thickened, silent and oppressive as a gathering storm. Elena's chest tightened with a mix of anger and something deeper—an aching awareness of what he feared she might lose, what they both risked if she stepped outside his protection. This was more than safety. It was about the fragile line between control and care.

She clenched her jaw, fists curling at her sides, but the fight drained away from her shoulders like the last flicker of a dying flame. She gave him a terse nod, voice clipped, steadying with effort. "Fine."

Logan turned away, reaching for the door, but beneath her calm exterior a fierce pulse of determination gathered strength, dark and unyielding. She wouldn't be sidelined—not this time. Not ever.

The air between them crackled, raw and electric. Logan's jaw clenched, his voice low, tight with both fear and fury. "This isn't up for discussion."

Before either could speak again, a heavy knock rattled the safe house door. Logan stiffened, reaching instinctively toward his weapon, until a voice carried through—firm, familiar. "It's Nora."

Logan opened the door to find Nora flanked by two agents, their presence filling the threshold with urgency. Her eyes locked on his, sharp and businesslike. "We have a window. Convoy's staged. If we're going to Baltimore, we move now."

Minutes later, Elena was sliding into the back of a black SUV, the leather cold beneath her palms. Logan climbed in beside her, the door thudding shut like a gavel. Engines rumbled to life outside as the convoy pulled away from the safe house, headlights cutting through dawn's silver haze.

The Virginia hills unfurled around them, fields washed pale by moonlight, the countryside deceptively serene. But inside the vehicle, tension thrummed like a live wire. Elena sat rigid, hands clenched over the folder in her lap, Donovan's latest move weighing on her like a stone.

Beside her, Logan's presence was a shield—unyielding, silent, always scanning. Across from them, Nora scrolled rapidly through encrypted files on a tablet, her clipped tone cutting into the quiet. "This warehouse is where Donovan's been cycling the money, pushing shipments, and scrubbing the trails. If it burns, so does half the case."

Elena leaned forward, voice steady but sharp. "Then we can't let it burn."

Nora's eyes flicked up, steady and assessing. "Agreed. But it won't be clean. Intel says at least a dozen men on site—armed. They'll fight to the last box."

Elena's stomach tightened, but she forced herself to nod. "Then we fight harder."

Logan's gaze cut to her, hard as steel. "You'll stay in the van. Vest on. Non-negotiable."

She met his eyes, her chin lifting with quiet defiance. The fight was far from over.

***

The warehouse loomed ahead, a dark monolith silhouetted against the night sky, its edges swallowed by shadows.

Inside the armored van, Elena's chest tightened, pulse hammering like a drumbeat in her ears. Logan's steady movements beside her were a faint anchor in the chaos—the scrape of his hands tightening her bulletproof vest straps, the slight hesitation as his fingers lingered just a moment too long against her skin. When his eyes found hers, the intensity was unmistakable—firm and protective, laced with an unsaid plea that twisted her stomach and held her breath hostage.

"Stay here," he commanded, voice low and unyielding. "Wait for me."

She nodded, taut and silent, the weight of his words settling over her like a yoke. Her hands clenched at her sides, a war raging inside—every instinct screaming to break free, to act, defy, move. Yet she remained frozen, bound by his command, even as the heat coursing through her veins threatened to ignite.

Bristling, she fought the growing fire of frustration. Logan didn't get to decide for her—not this time. But she swallowed the words, watching him and the others melt into the darkness, swallowed whole by the looming warehouse.

Minutes dragged, time dilating under the suffocating silence of the van. Her breath came shallow, every creak or whisper outside jolting her nerves into sharp alertness. Beside her, the young agent shifted restlessly, his nervous energy palpable as he fumbled with the controls.

She forced her gaze onto the monitors—grainy feeds flickering with uncertain shadows—but her mind refused to focus, stuck on Logan, the warehouse, on the unshakeable truth: she wasn't made to sit idle while everything she'd poured herself into teetered on the edge.

"Any update?" she asked, leaning forward slightly, voice steady despite the thrum of adrenaline hammering through her.

The agent glanced sideways, eyes not quite meeting hers. "Not yet," he muttered absently, fingers twitching over the buttons.

Seizing the moment, Elena leaned closer, breath steadying as she forced the wordless command. "Look—south side. Movement there, isn't there?"

He snapped his attention to the screen, eyes narrowing in concentration.

Without hesitation, Elena caught her chance. In the brief instant his focus shifted, she slipped from the van like a ghost, heart slamming against her ribs. The cold night air struck her bare skin as she melted into the shadows, every step weighted with urgency and defiance. The world outside was vast and silent, but inside her, the fight had already begun—whether Logan approved or not.

***

The cold night air bit sharply at Elena's cheeks as she crept toward the warehouse, each breath escaping her in shallow, rapid bursts that fogged faintly in the darkness. Every step felt heavier than the last—her boots muffled against gravel—but the distant crack of gunfire and raw shouts from inside sent jolts through her, making her flinch. And yet, with every roar of chaos, her resolve only hardened. She couldn't — wouldn't — stay hidden any longer. She had to act.

Slipping through a narrow side entrance, the shadows swallowed her whole, swallowing the world outside. The vast interior yawned open before her—endless towering shelves draped in darkness, mingling with the harsh, acrid bite of metal and dust. Her heart pounded thunderously in her ears as she pressed forward, hugging the shadows, ducking behind a stack of crates. Her eyes flicked nervously toward the far end where Logan and the team exchanged rapid-fire with Donovan's men.

Logan moved like a force of nature—his every motion precise, lethal, honed by countless battles. Yet amid the clamor, he paused for a heartbeat, scanning wide, then — lightning fast — his eyes locked onto hers.

"Elena!" His voice sliced through the noise, a raw blend of fury and panic that knocked the air from her lungs.

Before she could respond, a guard emerged silently behind her, and the world exploded into a blur of sound and motion.

"Elena, get down!" Logan barked; urgency sharp as a blade. But she barely registered the command before he was charging forward, firing with lethal intent at another attacker closing in.

A cold wave of reality crashed over her presence there—uninvited, dangerous. Logan's eyes flashed fire as he reached her, hands gripping her roughly but protectively, yanking her down behind the crates. His face hovered inches from hers, voice rough and fierce: "I told you to stay in the van!"

"And I told you I'm not sitting this out!" Elena shot back, her voice cracking with the raw, desperate emotion she could no longer keep locked away.

His jaw clenched tight, words caught on the edge, before a new throng of guards surged forward, shadows alive with threat. Logan's reaction was instant—he shoved her behind him, body stiffening into an unyielding wall as bullets screamed past, hammering the crates with deafening thuds.

Elena's heart raced, adrenaline flooding her veins as she watched Logan—a tempest of precision and fury. Every pull of the trigger, every sharp, calculated step, carried a fierce desperation beyond simple survival—a vow etched into muscle and bone to keep her safe.

And for a sliver of time, amid the fire and chaos, the truth crystallized: he would do anything to protect her. Yet here she was, unyielding, fighting beside him—just as determined, just as fierce—to see it through.

* * *

Gunfire and shouted commands blurred into a roaring chaos that hammered against Elena's senses. Her pulse thundered in her ears, panic clawing at her throat, but the moment offered no room for hesitation. Logan yanked her roughly to her feet, his grip firm but not unkind.

"We're leaving. Now," he barked.

Elena planted her feet stubbornly, every muscle taut with defiance. "Not without the evidence."

His jaw tightened, tension radiating off him, but before he could argue, Nora's voice crackled sharply through the comms. "We've got it. Fall back to the van! Move, move!"

Adrenaline surged, and they ran—bullets pinging and ricocheting off metal and wood like deadly percussion. Each sharp crack echoed through Elena, making her flinch as she wove through the labyrinth of crates. The weight of her vest dragged against her breath, legs burning with every desperate sprint.

The exit was just ahead—then a shadow lunged out. A rough, crushing impact slammed Logan to the ground. Elena's breath hitched, time fracturing for a split second as primal instincts screamed at her to flee. But Logan was pinned beneath a snarling guard, struggling fiercely.

Her eyes flicked to a crowbar half-buried in debris nearby—a cold, hard lifeline. Without a second thought, she snatched it up, swinging with raw desperation. The metal connected with a sickening crack against bone. The guard crumpled in a heap.

Logan shoved the lifeless weight off, pushing himself upright. His eyes locked onto hers, dark and fierce. "You're

insane," he muttered, but beneath that was a spark—
something dangerously close to pride.

"No time," Elena snapped, seizing his arm and hauling him
toward the exit.

The pounding footsteps of reinforcements chased them, but
she didn't dare glance back. The van glimmered just ahead
beneath the cold slice of moonlight. Safety was close—for
now. They only had to reach it.

***

The van lurched forward as the team piled in, Nora clutching
the secured case to her chest like a lifeline. Logan slammed
the doors shut, his breath still harsh and uneven from the
chaos they'd escaped.

"You could've been killed," he said, voice taut, threadbare
beneath the restraint.

Elena met his gaze, voice edged with fatigue and defiance.
"So could you. But sitting there wasn't an option."

His stare burned into her, layers of anger and relief tangled
with something she couldn't quite place—something
quieter, more vulnerable. He exhaled sharply, running a
hand through his tousled hair. "You're impossible."

"And you're overbearing," she shot back, a ghost of a smile
tugging at her lips.

An electric silence settled between them, thick and
unresolved, like a storm rumbling on the horizon.

Outside, the van sliced through the dark streets, its engine's steady hum a sharp contrast to the storm raging inside Elena. Her pulse hammered stubborn and loud, adrenaline gradually melting away to reveal the gnawing dread pooling low in her gut. She wrapped her arms tightly around herself, haunted by the memory of Donovan's men closing in, the echo of gunfire replaying relentlessly inside her head. The danger wasn't behind them—it pressed closer, invisible but unyielding.

Nora's voice broke through the tension, clipped and businesslike. "We'll be at the field office in ten. The tech team's ready to start digging."

Elena forced her thoughts to focus, voice steady despite the churn inside. "How long before we have anything we can use?"

Nora's jaw clenched, the weight of uncertainty pulling tight across her face. "Depends. If Donovan slipped up, we'll see it fast. If not… we could be looking at a long haul."

Elena shook her head, breath short with urgency. "We don't have the luxury of time."

Logan turned toward her, his voice firm but measured. "It's more than we had yesterday. We take one step at a time."

She nodded, but the unrest lingered, clawing at her calm. They weren't safe. Not yet. Not by a long shot.

Chapter 12: Piecing It Together

The FBI field office buzzed with relentless urgency, agents moving briskly beneath harsh fluorescent lights that flickered like the pulse of a city under siege. Elena followed Logan and Nora into a secure conference room, but her steps faltered as she took in the sprawling web of diagrams plastered across the wall. Her name was circled in red, linked to tangled threads of fabricated accusations and conspiracy theories—a meticulously crafted smear campaign designed to bury her before the truth could surface.

Her chest tightened, breath hitching. "We're fighting on two fronts," she said, voice steady but edged with steel. "Proving my innocence—and tearing down Donovan's network. Lose grip on either, and it's over."

Nora nodded grimly. "Clearing your name's paramount. Once the public doubts you, everything else collapses."

Elena swallowed hard, the sting of betrayal sharp. Donovan wasn't just trying to silence her; he aimed to shatter her credibility before she could expose his rot.

Logan crossed his arms, jaw clenched. "We can't just play defense. This smear campaign is his smokescreen while he tightens his grip. If we don't strike fast, he becomes untouchable."

Elena's eyes traced the chaotic maze on the board. Something about it felt too deliberate—too rehearsed. "He's confident, almost cocky. Like he knew we'd get this far. There has to be a backup plan."

Before anyone could speak, Nora's phone buzzed sharply. "I need to take this." She stepped out, leaving Elena alone with Logan.

The heavy silence settled, but Logan's quiet voice cut through, steady and unwavering. "This isn't your burden to carry alone. Donovan's actions aren't your failure."

Her gaze dropped; voice tinged with regret. "I trusted the wrong people. I let this happen. Now, I have to fix it."

Logan stepped closer; his presence solid. "You're not doing this alone. We'll take him down. Together."

Her resolve wavered, flickering like a candle in a draft—then steadied as she turned back to the wall of truths.

Later, the Middleburg safe house pulsed with frenzied energy. The living room was buried under maps, files, scattered notes—a battlefield of paper. Elena paced, mind racing. "We're close. I can feel it. But something's missing. It's like we're circling, not striking."

Logan flipped through a folder; eyes sharp. "If there's a thread, we'll unravel it. Donovan isn't untouchable."

Elena froze mid-step as a memory surfaced, sharp as glass. "Grant. Congressman Grant. Last year, he mentioned Donovan's offshore deals—shady contractors. I dismissed it then, but now…"

Logan straightened; interest piqued. "You think he kept records?"

She nodded slowly. "Grant documents obsessively. Notes, recordings—anything that ties Donovan directly could be in his files."

Logan's gaze sharpened. "Do you trust him?"

Her breath caught, hesitation flickering. Then firm resolve. "Yes. Integrity means everything to Grant. If anyone stands with us, it's him."

Logan grabbed his phone, fingers poised. "I'll call Nora. If there's anything, we can't waste a second."

As he dialed, Elena sank into a chair, thoughts swirling. The pieces were beginning to align, but Donovan's reach stretched wide and deep. Every step forward felt like walking a tightrope over a minefield.

Logan ended the call, voice steady. "Nora's on it. We'll hear back by morning."

Elena felt the tension coil tighter in her chest. "If Donovan catches wind of this—"

"He won't," Logan cut in, voice firm as steel.

His confidence wrapped around her like a shield. For now, it was enough.

***

The Crystal City skyline shimmered like fractured glass against the night, casting flickering reflections through the car's tinted windows. Elena sat stiffly in the passenger seat, fingers nervously twisting the strap of her bag as Logan expertly guided them into the shadowed embrace of an underground parking garage.

"Are you sure Grant will back us?" he asked steadily.

Elena glanced toward him; her voice low but steady. "I trust him. Grant's cautious—he weighs every word. But he listens."

They slipped inside through a dimly lit service entrance, taking a private elevator that hummed softly to a secluded hotel suite. The door swung open to reveal Nora pacing. Her sharp gaze softened ever so slightly at the sight of Elena.

"You holding up?"

Elena nodded stiffly, tension tightening at the edges.

Moments later, the door opened, and Congressman Grant stepped inside, eyes sharp and deliberate as they swept the room before settling on Elena.

"Congresswoman Delgado," he said curtly, the edge of accusation threaded through his tone, "You've stirred quite the mess."

Elena met his gaze with unwavering calm. "And you've been quick to believe the lies."

Grant faltered, momentarily disarmed, but before he could respond, Nora dimmed the lights and launched into a rapid-fire presentation. The screen flickered to life, bathing the room in stark evidence—offshore accounts, blackmail schemes, a tangled web of illicit financial trails. Then, crackling through the speakers, an audio recording: Donovan's voice, cold and calculating, admitting to framing her.

Grant's jaw clenched as the weight of their findings sank in. "I didn't grasp how deep this went." A flicker of guilt passed over his face. "I misjudged you."

"This isn't about me," Elena replied, voice steady. "Do you have anything concrete that can help us?"

Grant produced a worn folder from his briefcase, sliding it across the polished table. "Coded messages, financial transfers. I uncovered these months ago but only realized their significance recently."

Nora flipped through the documents, eyes widening in disbelief. "This… this could bring his entire operation crashing down."

The victory, however, was brittle and brief.

Logan's phone buzzed sharply, his expression darkening instantly.

"What now?" Elena asked, dread coiling in her stomach.

"Security breach. They know we're here."

Grant rose immediately. "I'll cover your exit."

Elena's heart hammered as Logan turned to her, voice low but unwavering. "Stick close. No mistakes."

They moved swiftly into the dim hallway, urgency propelling their steps. Donovan's retaliation was imminent—and yet, for the first time, the empire he'd built felt dangerously within reach.

But this was only the beginning. The fight was far from over.

Chapter 13: Embracing the Moment

The tension clung to them like a second skin as Elena and Logan hurried down the narrow service stairs of the Crystal City hotel. Each creak beneath their feet echoed sharply in the confined space, magnifying their futile efforts at silence. The distant hum of city traffic outside felt jarringly normal against the growing storm inside Elena's chest—every step pulling them closer to an unseen threat.

Logan's hand settled on the small of her back, firm but not overbearing. "Stay close," he murmured, voice low enough to be almost a part of the shadows. The sleeve of his other hand twitched near the concealed weapon beneath his jacket, a silent promise of protection—or danger.

Elena swallowed hard, trying to steady the frantic beat of her heart. Her mind darted through every shadow, every flicker of movement just beyond the peeling fluorescent lights. Had they been followed? Were unseen eyes tracking their every move? Nora and Grant had split off minutes ago, ensuring the pieces of Donovan's empire would soon crumble—but what if this was only the beginning?

At the alley's jagged edge, Logan swept his gaze, muscles coiled and ready. "Clear for now," he said, voice taut but controlled. "Let's move."

Stepping quickly into the alley's cold embrace, the sharp scent of rain before the storm mixed with the city's familiar blend of exhaust and distant cooking fires. Logan led them through backstreets, winding away from main roads where enemies or informants might lurk. Inside the car, the dim dashboard lights traced contours of his sharp features, eyes flicking to the rearview mirrors with practiced vigilance.

Elena clutched her bag tighter, fingertips white. The familiar skyline blurred as they left Crystal City behind, the looming spires gradually replaced by Middleburg's softer outlines. There was safety here—or at least the illusion of it— wrapped in the shadows of the safe house.

The building's silhouette emerged like a beacon in the growing darkness, its worn edges softened by the amber glow of porch lights. As they entered, Logan moved efficiently, double-checking every lock before arming the security system with deliberate care. Then he turned to her, the weight of what was to come settling between them.

"We've got tonight," he said, voice low but steady. "Tomorrow... everything changes."

Elena met his gaze, emerald eyes sharp yet vulnerable. The words hung in the air, heavy with unspoken fears and promises. She felt the tremor beneath her composed surface—fear tangled with something deeper, something raw and urgent.

"Tonight is ours," she breathed, the steady rhythm of her voice masking the tremors beneath.

Logan's fingers cupped her cheek, thumb tracing a gentle path over skin still flushed from their escape. "Then let's make it unforgettable," he said, tone soft but charged.

Together, they moved through the dim hallway, the flickering candlelight casting long shadows and bathing their surroundings in warmth. Logan's silent attention to detail was unmistakable—the plush rug underfoot, the soft linens on the bed just beyond, the faint scent of lavender and sandalwood in the air.

The bathroom door creaked open to reveal a sanctuary of calm. Candles flickered at varied heights, casting dancing patterns that played on the steam curling from the clawfoot tub. The antique piece was more than a fixture—it was a promise of respite, filled with water warmed to just the right temperature and scented with oils that teased the senses. The lavender mingled with delicate hints of jasmine, soothing Elena's frayed nerves more than words could.

Elena stopped short, her brows knitting in surprise. "Logan…" she breathed, turning to him. "When did you have time to do all this? How did you even—"

A shadow of a smile tugged at his mouth, his eyes softening in the candlelight. "I didn't need much time," he murmured. "I just needed to think about what you'd need most right now. I've spent my life planning escapes, securing routes, neutralizing threats. Tonight…" He reached past her, adjusting one of the candles with deliberate calm. "…I wanted to plan something that gave you a reason to exhale."

Her chest tightened, emotion knotting at the edges of her voice. For the first time in days, she felt the crushing weight inside her ease, replaced with something fragile, something warm.

Behind her, Logan's steady presence was reassurance incarnate. His breath brushed her ear as he whispered, "Relax, my love. Let me take care of you."

She turned slowly, eyes catching his reflection in the mirror—intensity mingling with tenderness. His hands found hers, fingers intertwining as he led her toward the bath with a gentleness that still betrayed his urgency.

Clothes slipped away as carefully as whispered secrets, silk falling aside to reveal skin kissed by candlelight. The tub's warmth welcomed her like a lover's embrace, water wrapping around her in soft waves. Logan knelt beside her, hands strong and steady as they settled on her shoulders.

His touch was skilled, deliberate, dissolving tension locked deep in muscle and mind alike. "You carry more weight than you know," he murmured, voice a low hum that seemed to pulse through her veins. "Let me share that burden."

She exhaled slowly, eyelids fluttering closed as the pressure of the past weeks began to ebb. His hands moved with equal parts passion and reverence, fingertips tracing hidden paths over her arms, causing shivers to ripple beneath her skin. The intimacy in each lingering touch spoke volumes of unspoken promises and fears.

Leaning close, Logan's breath stirred the fine hairs at her ear as he whispered, "You're so beautiful—so alive when you respond."

Elena surrendered fully then, the warmth of the water mingling with the heat blossoming within her. His hands charted tender journeys over collarbones and along the delicate lines of her neck, finally cradling her face. His thumbs brushed her lips with such reverence they invited a kiss—and she gave one softly, tongues meeting in a quiet dance of yearning and trust.

"I want to please you, Elena," Logan's voice dropped to a hoarse whisper, heavy with desire. "Tell me what you need."

Elena's eyes fluttered open, the flickering candlelight casting his shadow over the curve of her cheek. Her gaze met his, a delicate tremor of vulnerability threaded through the simmering passion. "I want…" Her voice faltered, cheeks warming as she searched for the words that felt both urgent and fragile. "I want to feel you—every part of you."

Logan's dark eyes softened, a blend of desire and something deeper flickering within them—something protective, almost haunted. He rose slowly, the powerful grace of his frame filling the space between them. His hand cradled the nape of her neck, steadying her as he lifted her from the bath, water droplets trailing down her skin like liquid stars in the candlelight. Her legs wound instinctively around his waist, their bodies melding skin to skin, warmth meeting warmth.

"I've wanted you since that first glance," he admitted, his voice roughened by emotion he rarely let surface. "Every thought since has been about this—about you."

Her hands found his chest, pressing against the steady thrum of his heartbeat—a cadence that somehow matched the wild rhythm within her own. Their lips met again, soft at first, then deeper, tongues weaving in a slow, intimate dance that unraveled months of tension and unspoken longing.

Logan carried her effortlessly toward the bed, his arms a fortress of strength and tenderness. As he laid her down, the candles flickered shadows across the room—shadows that danced with the quiet urgency humming in the air.

He paused at the edge of the bed, eyes drinking in the sight of her—every line and curve alive with anticipation. Slowly, deliberately, he peeled away his clothing, revealing a body honed by discipline and hardship, muscles rippling beneath bronzed skin. Elena's breath hitched as her gaze traced the hard length straining with shared need.

"Come to me," she whispered, voice low and urgent, "I want to taste every part of you."

He joined her without hesitation, the heat of his skin igniting hers as their bodies melded in the soft glow. Her hands explored the ridges of muscle along his back, memorizing him as if for the first time, while her legs parted, inviting him closer.

Logan's lips traced a path from her neck downward, each kiss a promise, each touch stoking a fire that roared beneath her ribs. His tongue teased, gentle and demanding, as his warm breath ghosted over her skin.

When he reached her breasts, Logan's attention deepened—slow, reverent worship that made her arch instinctively into his touch. His fingers gripped her thighs, sending a thrill of anticipation through her. He positioned himself at her entrance, his breath hitching as he paused, searching her eyes for permission.

"Tell me, Elena," he whispered, voice taut with longing, "say you want me."

Her gaze locked with his, wide and unguarded. "I need you. Now."

With a steady, determined motion, he entered her—and she gasped, body blooming around him. Logan remained still for a moment, allowing her to adjust, the unspoken tenderness weaving through the urgency in his eyes.

Then he moved—slow and sure at first, drawing out every sensation, every whispered sigh that escaped her lips. Each withdrawal barely breaking contact, every plunge a meditation on desire and trust.

Her hands dug into the sheets, heart pounding, body rising to meet his. The sound of their skin—a rhythmic, primal drumbeat—filled the enclosed space alongside their tangled breaths.

"You feel incredible," Logan groaned, voice ragged. "So tight, so alive."

Elena's nails grazed his shoulders, marking him with white-hot urgency. "Harder," she begged, voice trembling with need. "Please."

He responded without hesitation, gripping her hips as he deepened and quickened his thrusts. Their bodies moved in a fierce harmony, the heat rolling higher, a tension coiling tighter inside her.

"I'm close..." she whispered, voice fragile and breathless. "So close."

Her words shattered his remaining control. Logan's movements became frantic, raw, desperate—his hips pounding a wild tempo as his own release surged forward.

Elena's body convulsed beneath him, waves of pleasure crashing and breaking until she cried out his name, trembling with the force of it. He followed, his climax shuddering deep within her, their bodies locking in a final, fierce embrace.

The world softened as their heartbeats slowed, breaths mingling in the afterglow. Logan collapsed beside her, muscles slack but still warm, pulling her close so their skin pressed together, slick with heat and promise. His lips brushed her forehead, a tender touch that spoke more than words.

"Tonight was…" he began, voice rough with emotion.

"Perfect," Elena finished, a satisfied curve lifting her lips.

For this night, they had each other every raw moment to reach beyond the looming storm that waited just beyond the fragile safety of their haven.

***

The first pale light of morning slipped through the gauzy curtains, stretching long fingers of soft gold across the quiet room. Elena lay nestled against Logan's warm chest, her fingers tracing slow, absent patterns over the steady rhythm of his heartbeat—a fragile tether in the calm before the storm. Outside, the faint rustle of leaves and the distant call of a morning bird whispered the world's return, but inside, time seemed suspended.

For tonight, they had carved out a sanctuary—brief and precious—where worries and threats melted into the shadows. Yet beneath that fleeting peace, an unspoken tension lingered: the storm waiting beyond the walls, dark and relentless.

Elena breathed him in—the subtle scent of cedarwood on his skin, the steady warmth radiating through his body—and in that quiet intimacy, she found a fortress of strength.

Their fight was far from over. But, cradled together in the quiet dawn, they were ready to face whatever came next. Side by side.

Chapter 14: The Beginning of the End

Elena's gaze lingered on the windowpane, where the late-afternoon sun painted thin ribbons of amber across the worn countertops of the safe house's modest kitchen. The kettle's soft whistle had long since faded into silence, and her untouched coffee sat cooling on the table, its surface dulled with neglect.

Across from her, Logan leaned back in his chair, eyes sharp and restless, flicking intermittently between her and the door—a sentinel in a house that promised safety but whispered of ever-present danger.

She finally broke the silence, her voice barely above a whisper. "Do you think Nora got all the evidence to the right people?"

Logan's gaze softened for a fraction of a second before hardening with resolute assurance. "Even if there's a delay, what we've already sent is enough to bring Donovan down for good." He paused, studying the lines of exhaustion etched across her face. "Grant's files… they're just the final piece."

A flicker of hesitation crossed Elena's eyes—the weight of responsibility pressing down on her like a tangible thing. But beneath it, a simmering resolve held firm.

Logan's voice dropped to something gentler, almost coaxing. "You've done more than enough, Elena. Let's go to eat. You'll need strength for what's coming."

The warmth in his words tugged at her defenses, and slowly, she shifted her attention from the gathering storm beyond the walls back to the small, fragile moment between them—a brief, quiet reprieve before the fight resumed in full.

***

The diner hummed with a comfortable warmth, silverware clinking amid low conversations. The rich scent of bacon and onions mingled with fresh coffee, curling around Elena like a fragile reminder of normalcy. She sat tucked into a corner booth, the untouched food on her plate cooling under the harsh overhead light, a heavy knot tightening in her chest from the days that felt both endless and impossible.

Above the bar, the television flickered, casting blue-tinged light over the worn wood and weathered faces. Conversations dipped into silence as patrons instinctively turned toward the screen.

"In a series of coordinated raids overnight, the FBI has arrested several high-ranking officials linked to Congressman Donovan's criminal network," the reporter announced, voice steady but urgent.

The footage played: agents storming opulent estates, seizing files, hacking devices, their movements swift and methodical. Then Donovan appeared—hands cuffed, suit rumpled but defiant, eyes sharp and scanning the throng of reporters like a cornered wolf weighing prey.

Logan exhaled, leaning back with a slow, satisfied smile. "Not quite the untouchable kingpin anymore," he said, a hint of triumph edging his tone.

Elena's fingers fumbled with a napkin in her lap, twisting it absently. Relief felt fleeting, fragile. "It's not over," she whispered, her voice tight with warning.

The reporter continued, "Congressman Donovan released a statement calling the allegations baseless and politically motivated. He vows to fight back and clear his name."

The screen cut to Donovan resisting the guards, flashing a venomous gaze directly into the camera. His voice was low, cold as steel, sending a shiver down Elena's spine.

"To those who believe this is the end," he declared, voice laced with menace, "you've only just begun to see my wrath. Every person who crossed me will pay. Mark my words—this is just the beginning."

The diner erupted in murmurs and cautious cheers—small bursts of hope rippling through the crowd. But to Elena, Donovan's words were no empty noise; they were calculated weapons, designed to fracture and intimidate.

Logan's hand found hers, grounding but tense. "He's bluffing," he said, though doubt edged beneath his confidence. "Desperation makes people dangerous."

Her eyes stayed fixed on the screen. "And what if he's not? Men like Donovan don't surrender quietly. He's got allies, resources hiding in the shadows. His followers won't fade away just because he's in cuffs."

Logan's grip tightened. "The FBI has him cornered. They've got the evidence. He's lashing out because he knows the walls are closing in."

But Elena's gut told her otherwise. Donovan's gaze through that camera wasn't defiance—it was a promise.

***

The evening air was sharp when they stepped out of the diner, autumn wind curling around Elena with a chill that seemed to bite straight through her. The street was quiet, too quiet, the glow of the streetlamps stretching thin shadows across the pavement.

"Something's wrong," Logan muttered, his body tensing, hand brushing against the concealed weapon beneath his jacket.

Elena's heart jumped. "Are we being watched?"

His eyes scanned the dark edges of the street. "Let's not wait to find out."

The drive back was taut and deliberate, Logan urging the agent at the wheel to take backstreets and detours. The silence in the SUV was heavy, broken only by the low hum of the engine. Donovan's words echoed again and again in Elena's mind: This isn't the end. It's only the beginning.

When the safe house came into view, its silhouette dark against the night sky, Elena felt both relief and dread in equal measure. Logan swept the perimeter as always, sharp and meticulous, before signaling her inside.

***

Nora was already waiting, her energy restless, sparking in the dim lamplight. She paced near the battered wooden table, her fingers drumming a sharp rhythm against its surface.

"We need to talk," she said, gesturing them over. Elena dropped into a chair, weariness pulling at her bones.

"Donovan's arrest is everywhere," Nora began, voice clipped and urgent. "But your name—yours—is still being dragged through the mud. If you don't push back, his allies will keep poisoning the narrative."

Elena's stomach tightened. "How do I fight shadows and whispers?"

Nora's jaw set. "You shine light. We hold a press conference. Release what we can from the evidence. Tell your side before Donovan's network spins theirs."

Logan cut in, voice low, cautious. "That paints a target squarely on her back."

"She's already on that target," Nora snapped, her gaze flashing. "Silence just hands Donovan the reins. Control is power—he'll keep wielding it if we let him."

Elena looked between them—the fierce protectiveness in Logan's eyes, the relentless determination in Nora's—and felt the pressure close around her chest.

Her breath steadied. "I'll do it."

Logan leaned closer, voice quiet, edged with care. "Are you certain? This isn't just about clearing your name—it's survival."

Her eyes lifted, fierce despite the exhaustion. "If I stay silent, Donovan wins. That's not an option."

Nora's expression softened briefly with respect, then she pulled out her phone and began firing off calls, already setting the wheels in motion. "I'll handle logistics," she said briskly. "We'll have media ready within twenty-four hours."

She glanced back once at Elena, her features hardening again. "Get some rest. Tomorrow everything changes." Then she swept out, her exit as sharp and sudden as her arrival.

***

Silence filled the safe house once more. The weight of Nora's words pressed heavy, but so did the gravity of Elena's choice. She rose and paced the worn carpet, practicing fragments of her statement under her breath. The words wavered at first, fragile—but with each repetition, her voice grew stronger, more certain.

Logan leaned in the doorway, watching her quietly. "Do you think I'm doing the right thing?" she asked finally, her voice raw.

"You're doing what you've always done," he said simply. "Fighting for what's right, even when it terrifies you."

Her eyes shimmered with fatigue. "I'm terrified."

He moved closer, sliding beside her on the sofa, his hand finding hers, warm and steady. "You're also the bravest person I know. Whatever tomorrow brings, I'll be right here."

Her head rested against his shoulder, the simple weight of him grounding her as the storm raged outside.

***

The night stretched long and sleepless. By the time the first pale streaks of dawn pierced the horizon, Elena sat at the window, her reflection faint in the glass. Donovan's threats still looped through her thoughts, dark and venomous—but something inside her had hardened.

This wasn't the end. It was only the beginning of the fight to come.

Chapter 15: The Reckoning

The conference room buzzed with an uneasy energy, a charged undercurrent of whispered conversations mingling with the sharp clicks of cameras. Every seat was occupied, eyes narrowing, scrutinizing Elena as she stepped up to the podium. Her fingers curled around the lectern's edges—not just for balance, but as a tether to the resolve she struggled to steady within.

Her gaze swept the crowd—some faces betrayed curiosity, others plainly hostile. Weeks spent lurking in shadow, fighting to dismantle Donovan's poisonous web, had led to this fragile moment. Could she reclaim control of her own story? Could the truth outshine the lies?

She inhaled deeply; voice steady despite the crushing weight pressing down like a vice. "Thank you all for coming," she began. "I've called this press conference not just to address the allegations against me, but to expose the corruption eating away at our democracy's core."

The air thickened, anticipation hanging heavy like fog. A reporter in the front row straightened abruptly. "Congresswoman Delgado, if you're innocent, why have you been in hiding?"

The question stabbed through the silence. Elena met it head-on. "Because Donovan and his allies are dangerous. My silence was survival, not guilt."

A ripple of murmurs spread—skepticism etched into some faces. Another reporter leaned forward. "Doesn't your relationship with Donovan suggest complicity?"

Elena's jaw clenched subtly, grounding herself. "My interactions with Donovan were purely professional. The moment I uncovered his illegal actions, I took a stand. That choice made me his target."

From the back, a subtle movement caught her eye—Logan, alert and watchful, his gaze slicing through the crowd like a blade.

Pushing onward, Elena's voice strengthened. "This isn't just about me. It's about every person Donovan exploited, every shred of trust he shattered. Let me be clear: he did not act alone."

A shockwave rippled through the room. Questions erupted in quick succession.

"What do you mean?"

"Are you implicating others in Congress?"

"Who else is involved?"

Elena held her ground, unwavering. "The investigation continues, but rest assured—no one is above the law. All who are complicit will face justice."

The barrage of questioning continued, but then a sharp, cutting voice sliced through the room.

"You're lying!" someone shouted accusingly.

"Where's your proof?" another heckler growled.

The atmosphere shifted, tension rippling visibly as the murmurs swelled into heated murmurs. The crowd's mood darkened.

At the rear, Logan's body tensed; muscles coiled as his eyes locked onto the source of the disruption. His hand flicked a subtle signal toward security—silent instructions exchanged in a dangerous chess game.

Elena raised a hand, the gesture firm enough to still the restless crowd. Turning to face the hecklers squarely, her voice rang unwavering despite the tightening turmoil. "I hear your anger. Your frustration. I know what betrayal feels like."

Her gaze softened, drawing the room's attention inward. "But I have risked everything—my career, my safety, my reputation—to do what is right. If that's not enough, so be it. I will not be muzzled by lies or intimidation."

A collective breath seemed to pause, then a hesitant applause began—small at first, then swelling in quiet defiance.

But the reprieve was brief.

The lead heckler surged forward, flushed with fury. "You're part of the corruption!" he spat venomously. "You're no different from Donovan!"

A chair overturned with a crash, shouts spilling over as chaos erupted. Reporters scrambled back to avoid the maelstrom bursting loose.

"Elena, we have to go," Logan urged, his voice taut with urgency as he grasped her arm tightly.

Her pulse thundered and she shook her head. "I can't," she said, voice strained. "If I leave now, they'll say I'm running."

"You're not running," Logan said, locking eyes with her, steady and fierce. "You're fighting to live. Move."

***

The hallway just beyond the conference room stretched silent, its stillness a stark contrast to the storm of voices and chaos that still reverberated behind closed doors. The sharp click of Elena's heels echoed hollowly as she followed the security team, each step marked by a pounding heartbeat that drowned out the muffled uproar.

Inside a small, secured room, the cold air settled around her like a shroud. She sank heavily into a chair, fingers trembling despite the effort to steady them. The snarled insults, the crashing chair, the angry shouts—the cacophony of the mob's fury—played relentlessly behind her closed eyelids.

"You did everything you could," Logan's voice broke through the silence as he crouched before her, calm and steady like an anchor in a rising tide. "You stood your ground."

She met his steady gaze, but the shadow of doubt lingered in her eyes. "What if it wasn't enough? What if this only hands Donovan's allies more fuel to burn me with?"

"It was enough," he said quietly, conviction threading through his tone. "You didn't falter. You didn't let them shake you. That's what will linger—the strength, not the noise."

A sharp knock cut through the charged quiet. An agent stepped inside, the tension visible in his tight jaw and narrowed eyes. "The room is secure. The hecklers have been removed. But given recent events, we recommend postponing any further public appearances until we reassess the threat level."

Elena's body tensed. She rose abruptly, the chair scraping against the floor, eyes blazing. "No. I'm finishing the press conference."

Logan exhaled, the sharpness in his breath betraying the storm beneath his calm facade. "Elena—"

Her voice dropped; steel woven through every syllable. "If I walk away now, it becomes their victory. They take control of the story. I won't give them that power."

For a beat, he stared at her—reading the fire that refused to dim despite the danger.

"Fine," he finally said, voice low, measured. "But we do it my way."

***

When Elena stepped back to the podium, the restless tension in the room had softened but lingered like a low hum beneath the polished veneer. Eyes fixed on her, pens poised, cameras capturing every breath, the unspoken weight of expectation pressing down from every corner.

She inhaled slowly, grounding herself, the cool metal of the lectern steady beneath her fingers. "Thank you for your patience," she began, voice clear and steady, carrying the quiet authority forged from nights of fear and determination. "I understand that emotions are running high, and I don't take your concerns lightly. But truth is not shaped by anger or intimidation. It stands firm—unyielding, no matter the storm."

Her gaze swept the room, catching glimmers of skepticism, flickers of curiosity—and then, unmistakably, sparks of belief burning quietly in some eyes.

"I will not waver in my commitment to justice," she continued, each word deliberates, opening a space of hope amid the uncertainty. "Donovan's lies will not prevail. And I promise you—no matter how long it takes, the full truth will come to light."

A moment of silence stretched taut, fragile as glass.

Then, applause broke free—stronger this time—resonating through the room like a tide turning. It carried with it more than acknowledgment; it bore respect, a subtle shift in the air that even Elena could feel—as if, against all odds, the fight was no longer hers alone.

Chapter 16: The Aftermath: A
Dangerous Proposal

The press conference ended in a storm of shouted questions and flashing cameras, a chaotic blur that left Elena with barely a moment to catch her breath. She was quickly ushered through a narrow side exit, the weight of what had just unfolded pressing down like a physical weight on her shoulders.

Outside, Nora awaited by the waiting car, her expression a fragile blend of pride and concern. "You handled that brilliantly," she said quietly, her voice steady but rife with unspoken worries. "But you just stirred a hornet's nest that's about to swarm."

Elena barely registered the compliment before Logan's voice cut through the quiet tension—tight, controlled. "Especially with you dropping those hints about other names. That wasn't part of the plan."

She turned to him, the weariness sharpening into a flicker of irritation. "It needed to be said. The public deserves the whole truth."

Nora let out a resigned sigh as she climbed into the backseat. Elena slid into the front with trembling hands, running one through her tangled hair. "That also makes you a far bigger target now. Donovan's allies won't just sit quietly while you dismantle the last remnants of their empire."

Elena exhaled slowly, the knot in her stomach tightening. "Then we move fast. No time to hesitate."

Logan eased onto the road, eyes darting to the rearview mirror with sharp vigilance. His posture tightened, every muscle coiled beneath his calm exterior.

Elena caught the shift instantly. "What aren't you telling me?"

His eyes met hers briefly before flicking to Nora in the back mirror, distrust and calculation flickering behind his gaze. "We bait Donovan's allies into making a move. Force them to come at us before they're ready."

The words landed like a punch in her gut. Her pulse spiked.

"What exactly are you suggesting?" she asked, voice steady despite the rush of adrenaline.

Nora leaned forward; her tone measured but heavy with consequence. "He means we create a situation they can't resist—force their hand before they're fully ready."

Elena's stomach twisted, cold and sharp. Logan's gaze hardened without hesitation. "Yes. We decide when and where it happens. But we need tonight—every hour counts to prepare."

***

Under the thickening veil of dusk, they arrived at a discreet hotel tucked into one of D.C.'s quieter streets, the reservation secured through one of Nora's trusted intermediaries. The suite was modest—spartan yet functional, just enough space to serve as their fragile command center amid the mounting storm.

Elena watched Logan move through the rooms with practiced precision, every glance and gesture scanning for hidden threats. His sharp eyes lingered on every corner, every shadow. Only when he gave a curt nod of approval did Elena allows herself to exhale, though the tight coil of stress still gripped her shoulders.

Nora unfurled a large map of the city across the small table, her finger tracing a precise circle around an intersection near the Capitol. "This spot is perfect," she said. "High visibility, yes, but with just enough cover to make the right people feel bold, even careless. Tomorrow morning, we'll stage it so it looks like you're about to release more information."

Elena leaned closer, studying the map, her mind already racing. Nora continued, "We'll make it seem like a meeting—maybe a handoff of sensitive documents, or a rendezvous with a whistleblower."

She crossed her arms, skepticism tight in her voice. "And how do we make sure they believe that?"

Nora's eyes gleamed with unshakable confidence. "By tonight, whispers will reach the right ears. Subtle, but enough to unsettle them—to set the trap."

The weight of the plan settled heavily over Elena's chest. It was bold, dangerously so—but necessary. Her fingers closed tightly around the cold fabric Nora handed her—a bulletproof vest, stark and unyielding.

"You'll wear this tomorrow before leaving the hotel," Nora said firmly.

Elena flexed her hand, tracing the vest's contours, the hard promise of protection oddly comforting—and sobering. "And if they come for me?"

"They won't get close enough," Nora assured, voice low but unwavering. "We'll be ready."

Elena wasn't sure whether the words were meant to reassure or steel her resolve—or perhaps both.

Nora glanced at her watch, already gathering her things. "I need to start planting the seed tonight. We'll regroup in the morning." She met Logan's eyes. "Make sure she's ready." pausing at the door. She looked at Elena, then at Logan. "This isn't just a trap for them—it's a test for us." With that, she slipped out into the night, her absence leaving the air heavier, charged with expectation.

Elena bristled, tension radiating through her like a live wire, but the retort stayed locked behind clenched teeth. Nora caught the flicker of resistance, offering a brief, steadying glance before slipping toward the door.

Left alone, Elena stood in the thick silence of the suite, the vest still clasped tightly in her hands, the gravity of the coming hours settling deep in her bones.

***

"You should rest."

Elena barely registered the words. She stood by the window, the city lights bleeding softly into the dark night, her reflection blurring and mingling with the glow. Rest? In a world where tomorrow could end with her name whispered in tragedy?

She turned away, exhaustion settling deep into her bones like a cold weight. "How can I rest when tomorrow might be the night, I end up in a body bag?"

Logan crossed the room in measured strides, his voice steady, too certain. "That's not going to happen."

She folded her arms tightly, the barrier an anchor against the gnawing uncertainty. "You can't promise that."

"No," he admitted, voice lower, rougher, tinged with something raw—something that unsettled her more than fear ever could. "But I promise I'll do everything I can to protect you."

His words hung between them, heavy and unspoken. Elena drew in a slow breath, feeling some of the tension loosen its grip. "I won't pretend I'm not terrified," she whispered, the admission more fragile than she intended.

"It'd be strange if you weren't." Logan stepped closer, grounding her in a way that surprised her. "But we're ready—for whatever comes."

She nodded, forcing herself to anchor on the plan rather than the storm of doubt swirling in her mind. "It's just… a lot." After a pause, she added with a tired half-smile, "I could use a drink."

A ghost of a smile curved Logan's lips. "That, I can handle." Moving to the minibar, he retrieved a bottle of cheap wine and two glasses. "Not exactly top-shelf, but it'll do."

She watched him pour, her eyes tracing the steady motion of his hands—calloused, certain. A flicker ignited within her—not just desire, but a deeper yearning: for connection, for a moment's escape from the ceaseless calculations and looming danger.

He handed her a glass; their fingers brushed briefly, sending an electric spark coursing through her veins.

"To a successful operation," he said, lifting his glass.

Elena met his gaze, something unspoken exchanged in the heat of the moment. She raised her glass, voice just above a whisper. "To us."

They settled side by side on the worn sofa, bodies close but still a breath apart. The wine warmed her throat as the tension shifted—from the gravity of the mission to a silent, building anticipation. Her eyes drifted to Logan's lips—full, inviting—and a familiar ache stirred deep between her thighs.

Logan must have sensed it. His eyes darkened, hunger smoldering beneath the surface. Setting his glass aside, he turned to face her; the brush of his muscular thigh against hers sent shivers racing through her.

"You're incredible, you know that?" he murmured, breath hot against her cheek.

Her heart hammered fiercely as his strong hands settled on her waist, pulling her closer. "I'm just doing what needs to be done," she replied, voice fragile and breathy.

"No," Logan countered, his lips brushing the shell of her ear, trailing warmth that left goosebumps in its wake. "It's more than that. You're brave, determined, and damn sexy."

His words washed over her, stirring long-buried desires. She turned to him, their lips meeting in a slow, heated kiss. His tongue traced the contours of her mouth, tasting the sweet warmth of the wine and the fire simmering between them.

His hands explored unapologetically, sliding over the curves of her hips, the swell of her breasts beneath the thin fabric of her blouse. Elena arched instinctively, nipples hardening against the cloth, craving the softness of skin.

With deft fingers, Logan unfastened the buttons of her blouse, peeling it away to reveal a lacy black bra that barely contained her. He paused, breath hitching as his eyes raked over her, desire plain in the pressing hardness against his thigh.

"You're stunning," he whispered, voice roughened by need.

Elena's fingers curled around the hem of Logan's shirt, tugging it free from the waistband of his pants. Her breath caught at the warmth beneath the fabric as she peeled it slowly over his head. His sculpted torso came into view, skin glistening subtly with a sheen of desire under the soft light. She traced her fingers over the rigid planes of his abs, following the slow descent toward the curve of his hips, where her hands gripped the waistband of his pants with mounting urgency.

A low groan escaped Logan's throat, his head falling back in silent invitation as her touch explored him. His hands were equally deft, skillfully unclasping her bra and freeing her breasts. His palms cupped her gently, thumbs teasing her swollen nipples, sending shivers of pleasure rippling through her core.

"I want you, Elena," he rasped, voice thick with hunger and reverence.

She needed no further encouragement. Standing, she deftly worked the button and zipper of her skirt, letting the fabric fall softly to the floor. Logan's eyes darkened as she slipped out of her shoes, standing before him clad only in delicate black lingerie that both invited and defied.

With a surge of strength, Logan gathered her into his arms, the heat of his body melding with hers as he lifted her effortlessly. His lips found hers again, kisses deepening with growing urgency as he carried her to the bedroom. Gently, he laid her down, their eyes locking in a silent vow of pleasure and trust.

Elena's hands trembled slightly as they fumbled with his pants, eager to release him. He helped, swiftly shedding the last of his clothing, revealing his hardness, pulsing with raw need beneath her gaze. Her breath hitched, a swell of desire blooming within her.

Positioning himself carefully between her thighs, his hands settled firmly on her hips, guiding with a deliberate tenderness. Their bodies united as he entered her slowly, a ripple of pleasure coursing through Elena. Her head fell back, emerald eyes sparkling with intense sensation.

Logan's movements were steady and powerful, each deep thrust a measured rhythm that echoed through her body. Elena matched him, hands digging into his shoulders, nails tracing sharp lines against his skin as waves of ecstasy built uncontrollably.

Sweat slicked their glistening bodies; the scent of their passion mingling in the warm air. Logan's lips drifted to the sensitive curve of her neck, teeth gently grazing the delicate skin, his whisper low and intimate. "You feel incredible, Elena. So tight around me."

Elena's moans filled the room, a symphony rising with every stroke. Her fingers threaded through his dark hair, trembling as the tension coiled tighter and tighter until it shattered. "Logan, I'm close," she gasped.

His pace quickened, muscles tightening as need overflowed. "Come for me, Elena," he urged, voice rough and raw. "Let go."

In response, Elena's body convulsed around him, an explosion of pleasure that lifted her from the mattress as she cried his name. Nails raked his shoulders; her trembling release marked the air in a moment of raw surrender.

Logan groaned deeply, his own climax crashing through him as he throbbed inside her. A few more powerful thrusts followed, their bodies locked in a tangled embrace of sweat and desire.

They collapsed side by side, hearts hammering in tandem, breaths ragged yet content. Logan's lips sought hers again, their kiss soft and full of unspoken emotion.

As night deepened, they found solace in lingering touches and whispered promises. Their passion rekindled in slow, languid motions—each movement a silent conversation of trust and need. In the quiet moments before dawn, fingers intertwined, minds restless with the day ahead—yet cocooned in a fragile sanctuary borne of their love.

Outside, the first faint light threatened the darkness, carrying with it the inevitability of danger and intrigue. But in this bubble, Elena and Logan savored the warmth of each other's touch, their bond a steadfast beacon to guide them through the uncertain path before them.

Chapter 17: The Breaking Point

The morning broke under a shroud of gray clouds, pressing down on the city like the Unease twisted tight around Elena's chest, as tangible as the heavy, damp air that seeped through the cracked window. The smell of rain hung thick, mingling with the distant hum of morning traffic and the occasional sharp whistle of a vendor setting up for the day. Even the birds seemed subdued, their usual chatter muted into hesitant notes, as if the city itself held its breath in uneasy anticipation.

Through the windowpane, the waking world filtered in—the low rumble of engines, sudden blares of horns slicing through the quiet, faint snippets of conversation drifting past on the breeze. The normalcy clawed at her nerves, a cruel contrast to the tightening knot of anxiety coiling in her stomach.

Her movements became methodical, almost mechanical, as she dressed with deliberate precision. Each action was a small attempt to impose order on the chaos looming ahead. The bulletproof vest Logan had insisted she wear felt foreign beneath her blouse, its weight a constant and sobering reminder of the danger waiting outside. She pulled her blazer over it, fingers smoothing the fabric with steady, practiced hands—an unconscious ritual to calm the storm raging within.

In the main room of the suite, Logan stood by the window, framed in the pale, gray light of dawn. His silhouette was taut and watchful, his gaze sweeping the street below with the sharp vigilance of a man lifelong trained for threats both seen and unseen. When he turned, the steel in his eyes softened just enough, but the intensity beneath never wavered.

"You ready?" he asked.

Elena drew a slow breath, steadying it against the tightness constricting her lungs. "As ready as I'll ever be." The words came out firm, but beneath them thrummed a fragile undercurrent—fear, adrenaline, or perhaps a volatile mix of both she wasn't ready to name.

Logan stepped closer, his gaze locking on hers with unwavering conviction. "You've got this." His certainty felt like a lifeline—one she hesitated to grasp, yet in that fleeting moment, she let herself cling to it.

The drive to the Capitol was enveloped in silence, broken only by the steady hum of the engine gliding over asphalt. Logan's hands gripped the wheel with calculated control, every move deliberate, prepared for whatever might come. The familiar cityscape blurred past—monuments, busy streets, flags fluttering in the breeze—but none of it quelled the gnawing pressure tightening inside Elena's chest.

Her hands clenched in her lap, nails digging into the soft flesh of her palms. The sharp sting grounded her, anchoring her against the rising tide of doubt. The leather seat beneath offered a cool contrast to the heat prickling along her spine.

Each intersection they approached, felt like the steady countdown to an inevitable reckoning.

As they neared their destination, Logan's posture stiffened imperceptibly. His grip on the wheel tightened, knuckles whitening under his calm exterior. His voice dropped into a low rumble, edged with unmistakable warning.

"Stay alert."

Elena nodded, her throat tight enough to deny words, bracing herself for what lay beyond the car door.

The Capitol loomed ahead, its ivory dome stark against a brooding gray sky—a symbol of power that felt almost mocking given the corruption Elena was about to unearth. At its base, a swarm of agents and unmarked vehicles created a choreography of controlled chaos, their precise movements a fragile veil over the unseen forces chipping away at the heart of authority. The humid air buzzed with tension, pressing against Elena's skin like static before a tempest.

She forced herself to steady her breath as she stepped out of the car, each measured movement an act of defiance. Her pulse pounded loud enough to echo in her throat, but she willed her body to betray nothing. Agents flowed around her with effortless precision, their clipped exchanges and brisk gestures filling the space with restless energy. She tried to draw strength from their calm, but her fists clenched tightly at her sides—a silent war against the fear gnawing at her resolve.

Logan's sharp eyes tracked every subtle movement as he eased himself down beside her. "Keep your head high," he advised quietly. "Let them see your strength."

Her pulse thundered fiercely against her ribs, but she forced a nod.

The controlled chaos of security engulfed her senses. Dozens of agents lined the wide marble steps, their sleek earpieces catching glints of sunlight, their vigilant eyes sweeping the crowd from every angle. Their precise, methodical presence was oddly reassuring—and yet suffocating in its intensity. A restless sea of journalists and staffers pressed close behind sturdy barricades, a low hum of murmurs tangled with the sharp staccato of camera shutters filling the heavy air.

Then everything shattered.

A blur of frantic motion surged from the edges—a man lunged forward with terrifying speed, arm raised high, steel blade gleaming wickedly in his grip.

"Knife!" The word cut through the crowd like a gunshot.

Agents erupted into action, bodies colliding in a violent, tensed knot as they tackled the attacker mid-stride. The blade slipped from the man's grasp, skittering wildly across the pavement, spinning until it clattered sharply against the curb. Shouts and curses tangled amid the struggle as the man was pinned, his face pressed hard against the cold, unforgiving stone.

Logan shoved Elena forcefully back against the SUV, his body a solid shield, his grip locking iron-tight around her arm. "Stay with me," he growled, eyes darting, scanning rapidly for any sign of a second threat.

"I'm fine," she gasped, breath ragged and chest burning from adrenaline. She forced herself to stand taller, to hold steady as the cameras whirred relentlessly, capturing every tension-filled moment. She would not give Donovan's allies even a flicker of satisfaction in seeing her falter.

Within seconds, the danger was decisively neutralized. The man was hauled away, thrashing weakly as a dozen agents formed a protective barrier around Elena.

Logan's jaw was clenched so tightly it looked as if it might crack. "We're moving. Now."

They surged through the rotunda's expansive marble expanse, the echo of hurried footsteps snapping sharply against the polished floors. The grandeur of the place—with its towering columns and historic, frescoed murals—seemed muted beneath the pounding in her ears.

Finally, they slipped into a secured side office. Logan closed the door behind them with a firm click, his gaze methodically sweeping every corner before letting out a slow, controlled breath. He turned to her, his expression carved from steel and fire.

"You good?"

Her throat was tight, but she nodded. "I'm still standing."

"Barely," he muttered, pulling a small velvet-lined case from his jacket pocket. Inside, nestled delicately like something both fragile and lethal, lay the wire. He stepped closer, voice dropping lower, steadier. "This goes on you. From here on, everything you say matters. And everything they say matters even more."

She lifted her chin, meeting his gaze with unwavering resolve. "Do it."

His fingers brushed her collarbone as he clipped the microphone beneath her lapel. For a heartbeat, the world shrank to just the two of them—the warmth of his touch, the sharp focus in his eyes, and the silent vow passing between them.

The door cracked open and Nora slipped inside, eyes sharp, tablet clutched in one hand. "They're here."

Elena turned, searching Nora's face. "How did you even get them to agree to this?"

Nora smirked faintly, though tension pulled taut at the corners of her mouth. "Pressure and timing. We had leverage—Donovan's fixer exposed communications linking them to his offshore accounts. I dangled just enough talk of immunity to make them sweat. Told them it was in their best interest to meet with you, face-to-face, before this blows any wider." She tapped the tablet. "They think they still have room to maneuver."

"And do they?" Elena asked.

"Not anymore," Logan answered, his tone grim.

Nora's gaze flicked between them. "Security's tighter than ever after that knife stunt, but don't mistake it for randomness. Someone wanted to shake you before you stepped into that room."

Elena's fists clenched at her sides, nails digging into her palms. "Then they'll regret underestimating me."

When the agents gave the signal, Elena stepped into the corridor. The hall stretched long and gleaming, her footsteps echoing sharply against the marble. Every step she took was laden—with the weight of the wire hidden beneath her jacket, with the memory of the blade still gleaming in her mind, and with the heavy eyes of history pressing down from beneath the Capitol dome above.

At the far end of the corridor, the double doors stood waiting—heavy, foreboding. Two agents pulled them open in seamless unison.

Elena drew a slow, steady breath. Whatever lingering fear clenched her chest, she willed it to retreat deep inside. With heels clicking like gunfire against the polished floor, she walked forward—alone, unbroken, and ready.

This was it. No turning back.

Inside, the weight of expectation settled like a leaden cloak across her shoulders. The room was colder than she'd anticipated—whether chilled by the air conditioning or the icy stares of the three men seated behind the long-polished table, she couldn't tell. Their faces flickered with barely concealed irritation and practiced indifference, but the tautness in their rigid postures betrayed their true feelings. They did not want to be here.

Good.

Her heels clicked deliberately against the gleaming floorboards, the sharp staccato cutting through the heavy silence. One of the men shifted uneasily. She took her time crossing the space, letting each echoing step etch the gravity of the moment into the air. Her voice slid smooth and sharp-edged when she finally spoke.

"Gentlemen," she began, eyes locking on each in turn with unwavering challenge, "I trust you understand why you've been summoned."

A flicker of discomfort flared across their faces—swift, subtle, but unmistakable. She gave them no room for respite. Her words pressed forward, each syllable peeling away the layers of their carefully constructed shields.

"You were fully aware of Donovan's dealings," she accused, voice slicing through the room's heavy atmosphere. "The bribes, the threats, the trafficking—you were complicit. And now, with Donovan gone, you stand exposed."

Bering, the master of smug detachment, tapped a rapid rhythm against the table, his otherwise immobile expression punctuated only by a faint sheen of sweat at his temple. Carter, sitting stiffly beside him, cast a restless glance toward the door before snapping his attention back to Elena.

The third man fidgeted with his cufflinks, fingers twitching with betraying nervous energy.

They were unraveling.

Recovering first, Bering leaned back slightly, a thin, false smile stretched across his lips.

"Accusations, Congresswoman. Where's your proof?"

Elena barely resisted the urge to smile as Logan's voice crackled softly in her earpiece—low, certain, a steady anchor amid the storm. "Stay on them. They're breaking. Push harder."

She squared her shoulders and faced Bering directly, letting the silence stretch just long enough to make the smug man squirm. Then she struck, her tone sharp but controlled. "Proof?" she echoed, tilting her head slightly. "How about the offshore accounts linked directly to Donovan, funneled through your consulting firms? Or the shipping manifests connected to your so-called charities? You didn't cover your tracks as well as you believed."

The room shifted perceptibly. The confident facade they'd worn like armor cracked under the weight of her words. Unsettled glances exchanged around the table spoke volumes—the illusions of control slipping away.

For the first time since entering, Elena allowed herself a slow, steadying breath. She had them exactly where she wanted.

Bering leaned forward, defiance still burning bright. "Those accounts mean nothing without context. And good luck proving anything with those shipments." His tone sharpened, but it only spurred Elena to stand taller, to press her advantage harder.

Closing the distance, she moved closer to the table, every step measured and deliberate. "Tell me, Mr. Bering," she said, voice cold and precise like a scalpel, "how do you explain a $2 million transfer from Donovan's holding company to your account the day before the election?"

The reaction was immediate. The men stiffened, their masks cracking. Bering's face flushed—his arrogance faltering. "That wasn't—"

Before he could finish, Carter—the one with the worn gray hair—snapped beside him, frustration thick in his hiss. "Shut up, Bering. You're only making it worse."

"Worse?" Bering shot back, spinning to face Carter. "Don't pretend you're innocent. You were the one pushing fake bids on the defense contracts."

Carter's jaw tightened, eyes narrowing, but Bering was relentless. "And you didn't object when your cut came through, did you?"

Elena felt a surge of satisfaction as cracks deepened between them, their alliances unraveling beneath the relentless pressure.

Logan's calm voice whispered through her earpiece again. "They're turning on each other. Keep them talking."

She fixed her gaze on Bering, narrowing her eyes. "So, it's true. You all profited from Donovan's corruption. Finger-pointing won't save you now."

At the far end of the table, the third man threw his hands up in exasperation. "This is ridiculous! If Donovan hadn't dragged Bering into this, we wouldn't even be here. He's the one who pushed silencing her."

Bering's face twisted with fury. "I'm just saying aloud what everyone's thinking! If she hadn't started digging, none of this would have exploded like this!"

Elena held the silence, letting it stretch and suffocate the room with its sharp weight.

From the surveillance van, Nora's tone cut through the tension, urgent and commanding. "We've got enough. Move in now."

The door exploded open with a deafening crash that shattered the fragile calm. The suspects froze, panic flushing their faces. Bering jerked back, tipping over a water glass that splashed cool liquid across his lap. Carter shot a hand toward the table—a futile shield—while the third man recoiled, chair scraping jaggedly against the floor.

Armed agents stormed into the room like a tidal wave, their presence a violent contrast to the stunned silence before. Chairs scraped furiously, feet shuffled, and coffee mugs toppled, their spilled contents a final symbol of the defendants' unraveling grip on control. Nora's voice rang out crisp and commanding. "Hands on the table! Nobody moves!"

Elena felt Logan's presence beside her instantly, his form a shield as agents swarmed the table. The scene was almost surreal: men struggling, shouting, cuffed one by one. Bering snarled as his hands were forced behind his back. "This is entrapment! You won't pin anything on me!"

Nora's reply was icy and unwavering. "We don't need to pin anything. You just handed us everything."

Outside in the cold night air, adrenaline slowly ebbed from Elena's veins, though her resolve burned steady. She leaned against the cool metal of the SUV, the weight of the moment pressing in with quiet gravity as the breeze brushed her face.

"Did we get enough?" she asked, voice rough but steady.

Logan nodded, his gaze firm as ever. "More than enough. They imploded on their own. It's over for them."

Nora approached, a triumphant smile illuminating her face, satisfaction gleaming in her eyes. "You were brilliant in there, Elena. They walked right into the trap."

Elena managed a small, weary smile—one that didn't quite reach her eyes. This fight was far from over.

"It's not over yet," she said softly.

Logan's face softened; his voice low but resolute. "But it will be soon."

Chapter 18: A Victory and a Promise

Back at the Middleburg house, the atmosphere felt unexpectedly lighter than it had in months. The faint scent of red wine mingled with the earthy aroma rising from the rain-soaked countryside—a comforting cocoon of warmth wrapping around them. Even the flickering candlelight on the dining table softened the sharp edges of exhaustion, carving out a fragile space where relief, unfamiliar but welcome, could settle in.

Elena poured another glass for Nora, who'd arrived just after sunset. For once, her arms were free of the usual armory of documents and files, instead carrying only a bottle of wine and an exhausted, satisfied smile. Logan had shot a curious eyebrow at the lack of paperwork but said nothing, settling into his chair with his own glass in hand.

"To doing our part," Nora toasted, lifting her glass.

Elena met her gaze, clinking her glass gently against Nora's. "To making a difference."

They drank, the silence between them shedding its usual urgency and thick tension. Instead, it shimmered with a quiet reflection. The television hummed softly in the background, replaying coverage of Donovan's arrest—the sharp glare of flashing cameras as he was led away in cuffs, his once-confident posture faltering under the weight of public disgrace. Beneath the bold headline, a scrolling ticker detailed the breadth of the investigation: Millions in assets seized. Federal charges filed. Political empire crumbling.

The world beyond still buzzed with uproar and consequence, but for the first time in a long time, they weren't scrambling to keep pace with it.

"Feels strange, doesn't it?" Nora mused, swirling the wine thoughtfully in her glass. "Not strategizing, not fighting through the night."

Elena leaned back against the couch, eyes softening. "It does. But we did what we set out to do."

"Doesn't mean it's over," Logan added, tone gentle yet unyielding.

"No," Elena acknowledged, voice steady, "but for tonight, it's enough."

The weight of battles past lingered in the room like a shadow. Yet beneath it lay an undeniable truth: they had shaken the foundation. There would always be more to fight for, more to uncover, more corruption to dismantle—but this victory, however tentative, was worth honoring.

Nora exhaled a breath she hadn't realized she'd been holding, a small smile curving her lips. "Well, if we're officially off-duty for the night, I say we savor this rare moment of peace."

Elena smiled back, reaching for the bottle to refill their glasses. The fire crackled softly in the hearth, casting flickering warmth across the room. Rain tapped a steady rhythm against the windows—the world at ease, if only for a moment.

For the first time in months, they let themselves simply be.

Tomorrow, the fight would wait—but tonight, they rested.

***

The Capitol hummed with restless, almost electric energy as Elena stepped into the cavernous chamber. The crisp, deliberate click of her heels echoed sharply against the polished marble floor, slicing through the low murmur of whispered conversations like a blade through silk. The air hung heavy with anticipation—an intense, charged tension underscored by the subtle scent of polished wood and fresh ink that seemed to ground her amidst the swirling uncertainty.

All eyes immediately turned toward her. Some widened with genuine curiosity, others narrowed with skeptical calculation. The weight of those gazes settled heavily on her shoulders, yet she welcomed the pressure, drawing strength from it. Each deliberate, measured step she took toward the ornate podium felt like a small victory—a quiet, stubborn affirmation of the long and bruising road that had brought her to this moment.

The chamber itself was a mosaic of intent and doubt. Lawmakers straightened in their seats, some faces softened by tentative agreement, while others remained rigid, their skepticism carved visibly into furrowed brows and tense jaws. The warm glow from towering crystal chandeliers bathed the room, casting shifting shadows like dancers across the cold marble floor, heightening the solemn gravity hanging thick in the air.

Each footfall Elena took hushed a pocket of whispers, magnifying the stillness as all attention converged on her. When she finally reached the podium, she straightened with poise, lifted her chin with quiet defiance, and squared her shoulders as a steady wave of resolve radiated from her.

"Ladies and gentlemen," she began, her voice calm and steady despite the swirl of emotion threatening just beneath the surface, "we stand at a crossroads—a moment demanding accountability, not only for the wrongs that have been exposed but for the future we choose to build from here."

She laid out her vision with fervent clarity: specific, actionable reforms designed to dismantle the rot that had festered unchecked for far too long. Mandatory transparency measures requiring real-time publication of campaign donations and lobbying activities. The establishment of a citizen oversight committee tasked with monitoring federal contracts. She spoke passionately about protections for whistleblowers—the courageous few who dared to speak truth to power—and the urgent necessity of rebuilding the public's battered trust in their government.

Nods of assent rippled through the chamber, subtle signs of thawing resistance, while others remained impassive, their doubt casting long, ominous shadows over the room. The tension was palpable, a charged silence hanging in the air as Elena challenged her audience to rise above partisan divides and embrace the grueling, necessary work of restoring integrity to their institutions.

As she finished, a ripple of applause stirred—neither overwhelming nor unanimous—but charged with significance, a quiet signal that the path forward had begun, though the journey was far from over, fraught with challenges yet to come.

Stepping away from the podium, Elena felt the raw weight of responsibility press against her chest. Her gaze drifted upward to the gallery above, where Logan leaned casually against the railing. His expression was unreadable but steady—a silent pillar amid the storm. Their eyes met across the room, and in that brief connection, the clamoring noise of the chamber faded to a muted hum. He gave her a small, genuine nod, a rare smile tugging briefly at his lips—the first sign of warmth she had seen from him all day.

As Elena exited the chamber, the burden pressing down on her no longer felt like an anchor but a mantle she was ready to bear—fierce and determined, knowing full well that this was only the beginning of the fight, yet confident that they had laid the foundation for lasting change.

Chapter 19: Sentencing & Speech

The courtroom smelled faintly of varnish and old paper—a room built for memory and solemn reckonings. Elena sat on the second bench; palms pressed flat against her skirt to steady the tremble that threatened to betray her composure. Two rows ahead, Donovan sat rigid, his jaw cocked in that familiar defiance, but the usual shine in his eyes was gone. No entourage flanked him. No smug grin played for the cameras. He wore instead the gray suit of a man who had finally run out of doors to escape through.

Logan stood quietly along the wall near the aisle—close enough to catch her eye when needed, far enough to blend into the background. When her glance flicked back to him, he dipped his chin once with a muted reassurance: You're not alone.

The judge's voice rang out in an even baritone, reading the sentence—years, fines, restitution, supervised release—each word landing like a stone lifting from Elena's ribcage. Donovan didn't glance back as deputies moved toward him. He didn't look at anyone at all. That silence, somehow, felt like the deepest admission of guilt.

As the gavel fell with definitive finality, the gallery erupted—half whispers, half shocked gasps. Reporters slipped out like shoals of startled fish; cameras tucked away. Elena remained seated until the aisle was clear. When she finally rose, her knees steadied beneath her. Logan was already there, his presence a solid wall she could lean on or walk past. Today, she chose the latter—walking forward on her own strength.

Outside, the late-afternoon sun bathed the courthouse steps in warm, unwavering light. Microphones sprouted from gleaming metal stands. Red recording dots blinked to life. A dozen voices called her name urgently.

"Elena, do you blame the party?"

"Congresswoman, are you pursuing censure for his allies?"

"What do you say to donors who—"

She raised a steady hand—not to silence them, but to grant herself a measured breath. She had crafted the bones of these words on restless, sleepless nights. Today, she would no longer speak to the storm swirling around her, but directly to the people standing in it.

"Thank you," she began, her voice clear and resolute. "Today isn't about vengeance. It's about accountability. When public trust is sold off in back rooms and hidden behind burner phones, people lose faith—not just in one man, but in all of us. I ran for office to make it harder to hide power and easier to see the truth."

A hush fell—a quiet so profound it couldn't be caught by cameras, but was felt deeply by every listener present.

"We cannot fix corruption with headlines or sentences alone. We fix it with structure: transparent funding, open-bid contracts, independent oversight with real teeth. In the coming days, I will introduce the Clear Lines Act—a comprehensive package designed to disclose dark-money conduits, protect whistleblowers, and enforce meaningful penalties for violations. I am inviting colleagues from both parties to co-sponsor. If you believe sunlight is not partisan, join me."

She let her words settle like heavy seeds sown into fertile ground. The sun warmed the crown of her head like a benediction.

"To every staffer who was told to 'just look away,' to every voter who wondered if it was naïve to expect better—don't look away. Hold us accountable. Hold me accountable." Her throat tightened, but she didn't flinch. "Because integrity is only brave when it's inconvenient."

A murmur rippled through the crowd—soft, human-sized applause rising from somewhere beyond the barricades. Not a wave, but a genuine affirmation. Elena stepped back from the microphones as reporters surged with follow-up questions, but she quietly declined, moving towards the courthouse doors where the day felt noticeably quieter.

Logan fell in beside her without a word as they slipped around the colonnade and into the shade. The sudden stillness made her realize just how loud the months behind her had been.

"You did it," he said softly.

"We did a part of it," she corrected, the adrenaline finally ebbing away. "The rest is bills, committees, amendments—" She looked up at him thoughtfully. "The unglamorous war."

He smiled, small and real. "I've heard you're good at unglamorous."

They reached the side steps that fed into a small pocket park dotted with maples and a stone fountain. No cameras here. Just a pair of tourists tracing patterns in a guidebook and a toddler marveling at how far leaves could float on the water.

"I'm staying," Logan said, as if he'd been rehearsing the line and finally trusted it. "If you want me here."

"Staying?" She turned toward him, surprise flickering in her eyes. "In D.C.?"

"In your orbit." The corners of his eyes tugged with a hint of vulnerability beneath his usual professional calm. "I came here to be useful and leave clean. Then you… complicated the exit."

Warmth rose to her cheeks, unexpected and welcome. "And what does 'staying' look like for a man who doesn't like cameras or committee breakfasts?"

"Quietly," he said with a touch of dry humor. "I have a lead on a small security consultancy. Off-book threat assessments, digital hygiene for offices that don't even know the word 'metadata.' I can keep you safer without standing in every shot."

She exhaled, surprised by how deeply the offer steadied her. "You're not a distraction, Logan."

"Neither are you," he murmured, and the echo of an old conversation made them both smile softly.

A gust lifted a few leaves into their orbit. Elena reached for one but missed. "There's one more thing," she said, lowering her voice. "The drive Nora found in Donovan's storage closet—the one with the asset ledger. There are names that don't match any donor registry. Someone built a lattice under the floorboards."

Logan's posture shifted—alert, but not alarmed. "We follow it. Carefully."

"We follow it," she agreed. "But not today."

"Not today," he echoed.

They sat on the fountain's edge, sharing a silence that wasn't empty. Somewhere nearby, a church bell tolled five times. Elena thought of the constituents who had stopped her for photos, for prayers, and for angry questions she had to absorb and carry without breaking. She thought of the interns who still believed they could be the first generation to do politics gentler on the soul. She thought of the bill with its awkward name—one that would be mocked, then argued fiercely, then—if luck held—voted into being something that truly mattered.

"Walk?" Logan asked gently.

"Walk," she said.

They moved along the winding path, shoulders close but not touching. Around them, the city began to exhale—traffic slowing, office windows darkening, and the sky shifting toward a deepening copper hue. When they reached the corner, she paused.

"Come to the Hill tomorrow," she said. "I want you in the room when we draft the enforcement section."

"Is that an invitation or an order, Congresswoman?"

"It's insurance," she said with a small smile. "Against me getting talked into soft teeth."

He chuckled. "I'll bring sharper ones."

They crossed with the light. At the far curb, Elena's phone buzzed—a message from Valerie: three missed calls and a text with a single flame emoji and the words: you lit it up. Her laugh came lighter than she felt. She typed back quickly: we keep it burning.

Logan watched the exchange with the fond patience of someone learning to read her weather. "You hungry?"

"Starving," she admitted. "But if you suggest a steakhouse with a back room, I'm filing a grievance."

"I know a place with bad lighting, better pasta, and an owner who can't be bribed because he hates everyone equally."

"Perfect," she said.

They turned toward the avenue. A distant siren wailed and faded. Over the rooftops, the first star of evening fought through the city glow. Elena glanced sideways at him, felt the quiet yes of the moment settle like a soft promise deep inside.

Accountability wasn't a finish line. It was a discipline. So was hope.

She threaded her arm through his.

"Let's go write a better ending," she said.

"Chapter one," he replied.

They walked on.

Author's final note:

When I first sat down to write *Lines of Loyalty*, I thought I was simply chasing a story about power, corruption, and politics. But somewhere along the way, it became more than that. It became about courage when silence would be safer. About loyalty when betrayal is easier. About finding love in the middle of danger and realizing that sometimes the fight for truth is also a fight for your own heart.

This book is my debut, and writing it has been both terrifying and exhilarating. Every page carried pieces of me—the doubts, the persistence, the quiet hope that someone out there might see themselves reflected in Elena's determination or in Logan's relentless will to protect what matters.

If you are holding this book in your hands, I want to thank you. Your time and trust mean the world to me. Stories don't live without readers; they don't breathe without someone stepping inside their world. Thank you for stepping into this one.

Most of all, know this: while *Lines of Loyalty* tells its own story, it's only the beginning. The fire continues to burn, and the truth will demand to be heard in what comes next.

With gratitude and hope,

Starlynd Rivers

Epilogue

The bill was almost finished. Weeks of bruising debate, midnight revisions, and backroom deals had carved it into something Elena could finally stand behind—something that might outlast her. Something worth every scar it had taken to get here.

She stood at the lectern, the quiet thrum in her chest not from victory, but from the fragile nearness of it. For the first time in months, her body wasn't braced for the next blow. She was standing on ground she had bled to claim. And this time, it held.

"The measure before us," she began, voice steady though her throat was tight, "is more than legislation. It is a promise— that integrity still has a place in governance, and that we will not turn away from the abuses of power that nearly broke this chamber."

Her words rose into the silence. This wasn't triumph. It was survival stitched into hope, thread by trembling thread.

When she finished, the applause wasn't thunder. It was rain—soft, steady, falling on scorched earth. Not loud, but enough. Enough to seep into the chamber, into her bones, into every wound that had carried her here.

The gavel struck. The session moved on. But Elena felt the shift. The floor beneath her no longer trembled. It breathed.

Up in the gallery, Logan watched with the stillness of a man trained to disappear in plain sight. Their eyes found each other. He gave the smallest nod, but it was everything.

We made it. For now.

Outside, the air was soft, almost too gentle for a day that had carved history. On the terrace, the last cameras were retreating, leaving her with silence and sky.

Logan waited, leaning against the rail. His smile was unguarded, rare, and it pierced straight through her defenses. Something inside her chest—tied up for months—unraveled at the sight of him.

You were good," he said.

"I was honest." Her lips curved faintly. "Sometimes those look the same."

"Today," he said, stepping closer, "they did."

Above them, the dome gleamed—marble and myth, heavy with promises. A breeze caught her hair, and Logan tucked it back with a touch that lingered at her temple. His fingers trailed just enough to send a shiver down her spine. Gentle. Certain. A vow in the brush of skin on skin.

"You can breathe now," he murmured.

She inhaled—and the air slid into her lungs without a fight. The release was dizzying.

"Stay tonight," she whispered. "No politics. No plans. Just us."

His gaze darkened, slow and deliberate. "I'll clear my evening."

Their kiss met like a fuse sparking to life—slow, then hotter, certain, consuming. It wasn't desperation. It was claiming. The kind that promised more behind closed doors. The kind that said survival was not the end, but the beginning.

Then her phone buzzed.

Unknown number.

She almost ignored it. Almost. But instinct made her look.

Well done. We should talk before the embers catch. — L

Her pulse faltered. She tilted the screen toward Logan. In an instant, his easy warmth hardened into alertness.

"Could be noise," he said, though his eyes had sharpened. "But it feels like someone who watched you today."

"'Embers,'" she murmured.

"Someone wants you to feel seen," he said grimly. "That's step one to being steered."

She folded her speech into her bag, the paper suddenly heavier. "Do we answer?"

"Not from this phone. Not tonight."

They walked toward the exit. The Capitol dome loomed above them, pale against the darkening sky. Accountability was a promise she meant to keep—even as shadows gathered at the edges of her victory.

Logan reached for her hand. She let him take it.

Victory was not the ending. It was the door.

And beyond it, the embers waited.

But as they stepped into the street, a black sedan slid past, engine low and steady. In the back seat, a woman with dark hair and a faint European smile watched them through tinted glass. She raised her phone, snapped a picture, and sent it to a contact labeled only Mother.

The reply came instantly.

She doesn't know yet. Tell her the truth when the fire starts.

The sedan melted into traffic. Elena never saw it.

Inside the car, the woman scrolled to the attached image—zooming in, not on Elena, but on the man beside her. Her finger tapped his face. A second message appeared on her screen, this one from a different thread, marked with a government seal.

Asset confirmed. Embedded since day one. Clause 47 is in place.

The woman smiled faintly. "When the fire starts," she whispered, "he'll be the one to light it."

Somewhere, the match had already been struck.

One name.
One message.
One spark—
and the fire of truth begins.